VIA Folios 182

Benedetta in Guysterland

Published by Bordighera Press, an imprint of the John D. Calandra Italian
American Institute of Queens College, The City University of New York.

25 West 43rd Street, 17th Floor, New York, NY 10036

Library of Congress Control Number: 2025933768

The cover features the painting *Aeneas and the Sibyl in the Underworld*
by Jan Brueghel the Younger.

Benedetta in Guysterland was originally published by Guernica in 1993.

Publication © 2025, Bordighera Press
Text © 1993, Giose Rimanelli

VIA Folios 182
ISBN 978-1-59954-233-1

Benedetta in Guysterland

A Liquid Novel

Giose Rimanelli

BORDIGHERA PRESS

Contents

Theodore Raethke
to Benedetta Ashfield:

The wasp waits.
The edge cannot eat the center.
The grape glistens.
The path tells little to the serpent.
An eye comes out of the wave.
The journey from flesh is longest.
A rose sways least.
The redeemer comes a dark way.

Prefaces

Parody at the Border

Giose Rimanelli as Trickster, *Benedetta* as Missing Link

> Postmodern parody is both deconstructively critical and constructively creative, paradoxically making us aware of both the limits and the powers of representation.
>
> Linda Hutcheon
> *The Politics of Postmodernism*

> The trickster summons agonistic imagination in a narrative, a language game, and livens chaos more than bureaucracies, social science models or tragic terminal creeds; the comic holotrope is a consonance of narrative voices in discourse.
>
> Gerald Vizenor
> 'Trickster Discourse'

I first read the manuscript of this novel in 1987, shortly after having met Giose Rimanelli in Philadelphia at the 1986 American Italian Historical Association's conference.[1] When I finished it I told him he had to publish it. He replied, quite matter-of-factly, 'You will publish it.' And so, five years later, with the help and direction of Antonio D'Alfonso and Julia Gualtieri of Guernica Editions, another Rimanelli prophecy became true.

The first question that comes to the reader of *Benedetta in Guysterland* is why this novel is only now being published. After all, by 1970, the year it was written, Rimanelli was an internationally acclaimed writer who had published several very successful books in Italy that had been translated into eight languages (novels, such as *Tiro al piccione* (Einaudi, 1991), that are now best sellers, being rediscovered and republished as classics); he was a well-known journalist and cultural critic. Since 1961 he has been a tenured professor in American universities such as Yale, promoted on the merits of his writing, and not by virtue of his academic credentials. So why didn't he publish this novel right after it was written?

The answer to this question lies in the fact that Rimanelli did not write it for publishing; he did not write it for money; he wrote it for love, for love of literature and for his American friends whose responses he has included in the Appendix. The novel, to him, was simply an experiment in English, his first response to the demands of starting over again, from scratch, as a writer with a new language, a man of the world with a new toy. Yet while the language was new, his knowledge of literature and his knowledge of America was not. With a grandfather born in New Orleans, and a mother born in Canada, North America had entered his imagination long before his arrival in the 1950s. In fact, we can see those images forming in his earliest novels.[2] While born Italian, Rimanelli was destined to be the American citizen that he is today. *Benedetta* is the record of his divorce from his native culture which he chose to leave, and it is the result of his first two decades of immersion into American culture.

As writer Anthony Burgess noted in an introduction to *Alien*, Rimanelli's unpublished book of poems in English written between 1964 and 1970, 'Rimanelli is one of those remarkable writers who, like Joseph Conrad . . . have turned from their first language to English, and have set out to rejuvenate it in a way few writers could do who were blessed and burdened with English as their first language' (*Alien*, Poems, p. 244). Burgess knew Rimanelli's Italian work well and referred to him as 'the *enfant terrible* . . . who, in Italian has done remarkable and shocking things' (p. 244). As Burgess said, 'The nature of the business is to see Western civilization in decline, from the viewpoint of a sort of American who has brought, like Nabokov, all his European luggage with him and regards his primary devotion as belonging to the world, not to a mere segment of it' (p. 244). What Burgess said

13

about Rimanelli's earliest poems in English, applies as well to his first English narrative.

What I have to say about this work will not take the form of explication, Rimanelli shows us well enough how it is done in Appendix entry number four. My task is to situate this novel, published more than two decades after it was written, into the body of Italian/American literature. And *Benedetta in Guysterland* occupies a pivotal position in the history of Italian/American narrative as the bridge over the border between modernism and postmodernism.

Until this novel, we could not talk about a distinctive and visible Italian/American presence in postmodernism — there needed to be a product of the modernist project which serves as a bridge. The completion of such a project, in the eyes of Fredric Jameson, might be marked by parody, a form that, until *Benedetta*, had yet to emerge in Italian/American literature. It is interesting to note that until Rimanelli, the parody of Italian/American modernists has not been a form that Italian/American narrativists have turned to. Rimanelli's novel provides us with the missing link between Italian/American modernists and postmodernists. Because *Benedetta* remained unpublished, and thus outside the range of influence on Italian/American writers, we can only speculate as to how it might have contributed to a quicker movement from a modernist to a postmodernist Italian/American culture.

Benedetta in Guysterland is, without doubt, the most parodic text in Italian/American culture; it is the first Italian/American novel to, in Fredric Jameson's words, 'cast ridicule on the private nature of these [modernist texts] stylistic mannerisms and their excessiveness and eccentricity with respect to the way people normally speak or write' ('Postmodernism and Consumer Society', p. 16). While we are just beginning to see the buds of parody in Italian/Americana, due to the fact that more and more Italian/American authors are cognizant of the cultural products of the Italian, American and Italian/American cultures, parodies of Italian/American culture have long been products created by non-Italian Americans.[3]

The critic whose work on parody serves us well in our reading of this novel is Linda Hutcheon. Hutcheon sees parody as a vital form of expression of those marginalized writers.

> Parody has perhaps come to be a privileged mode of postmodern formal self-reflexivity because its paradoxical incorporation of the past into its very structures often points to these ideological contexts somewhat more obviously, more didactically, than other forms. Parody seems to offer a perspective on the present and the past which allows an artist to speak *to* a discourse from *within*

it, but without being totally recuperated by it. Parody appears to have become, for this reason, the mode of what I have called the 'ex-centric', of those who are marginalized by a dominant ideology (*Poetics*, p. 35).

Rimanelli knows the experience of life in the margin. Not only is he familiar with the margin between Italian and American culture, he knows the margin between Italian and Italian/American culture. It is this experience that has given him the perspective through which parody is possible.

While *Benedetta in Guysterland* is a novel written before its time, it has appeared, I believe, just in time. Giose Rimanelli's first published novel written in English fills a deep void (one that is perhaps unknown to many) in Italian/American literary history; that void is the cavity caused by the decay of a literary realism characteristic of the standard fare produced by Italian/American writers. For too long, those imaginations have been held prisoners by the psycho-social borders of the Italian/American ghetto. In other words, while the emphasis of most Italian/American fiction has been the Italian/American experience, most authors have been unable to gain a distance from the subject that would enable them to gain the new perspectives necessary to renew the story of Italian life in America. What Mario Puzo romanticized in *The Godfather* (1969), what Gay Talese historicized in *Honor Thy Father* (1971), Giose Rimanelli has parodied in *Benedetta*, and in that parody he has transcended the Italian/American subject by above all writing a book about literature through the same subject used by Puzo and Talese.

This novel, finally published more than twenty years after it was written, is Rimanelli's American *capolavoro*. If as Ben Morreale once said in conversation, 'An artist hides in his work with the hopes that someone will find him', then we need look no further than *Benedetta* to find a true Italian/American writer. Rimanelli is one writer who balances his life on the border of tradition and the *avant garde*. While we are all forever in debt to those who come before us, Rimanelli is one writer who not only acknowledges this, in this novel, but also transcends this debt by creating a fountain at which the future can refresh itself. This refreshment comes to us through his use of parody and satire.

Benedetta is first of all a parody, a form vital to the evolution of any literature. It is this parody that at long last enables the Italian/American narrative to find its way out of the medieval-walled labyrinth of modernism and into the wall-less maze of postmodernism. This novel turns gangsters into philosophers, by giving them a language they could never, in reality, ever possess, and in the same stroke, Rimanelli turns philosophers into accomplices as hit-men of ideas. Addressed by a young WASP woman to an exiled American gangster, the novel, in effect, also turns the reader into a gangster, for reading is after all one way of 'stealing' the work of another and adding it to our knowledge.

Benedetta demonstrates that one culture could not satisfy Rimanelli. More than an Italian, an American, or an Italian/American writer, Rimanelli is, in the tradition of Franz Kafka, Vladimir Nabokov, Jorge Borges and Gabriel Garcia Marquez, a *border writer*. Such border writers, in the words of Emily Hicks, demonstrate a 'multi-dimensional perception', the possibilities of inscribing a text with an awareness of the referential codes of both cultures who share the same border. While Italy does not share a physical border with the United States, Rimanelli represents the writer who is the cultural border crosser. Hicks points us to an explanation of the difficulties we face when we encounter a text such as *Benedetta*: 'The reader of border writing will not always be able to perceive the "logic" of the text at first. Nor will she be able to hear the multiplicity of discourses within a single language' (p. xxvi). And while Hicks concentrates the application of border theory on Latin American writers, her work serves well our reading of Rimanelli and other Italian/American writers. 'Border writing offers a new form of knowledge: information about and understanding of the present to the

18

past in terms of the possibilities of the future' (p. xxxi).

This is a notion similar to Hutcheon's perception of the way parody politicizes narrative: '. . . through a double process of installing and ironizing, parody signals how present representations come from past ones and what ideological consequences derive from both continuity and difference . . . parody works to foreground the *politics* of representation' (*Politics*, p. 93-4). Rimanelli's work, again in Hutcheon's words, is 'a form of ironic representation . . . doubly coded in political terms; it both legitimizes and subverts that which it parodies' (*Politics*, p. 101).

Incorporating America's obsessive fascination with the 'mafia', sex and violence, *Benedetta* tells the story of America's relationship with Italy and debunks the traditional stereotype of the Italian/American gangster (who, rather tellingly, ran the 'Mamma Mia Importing Company'), in a vital socio-political parody that shows that sex and violence are in fact displacements of each other. At the same time, the story told here is about change and the breaking away from roots that happens to all cultural border crossers. Through intricate pastiche, word play, the onomasticon understatement, the *tabula rasa* in expressing experimentation, *Benedetta* shows a way of making a truly great postmodern Italian/American novel. Rimanelli advances the Italian/

American novel by adding new dimensions to *Italianità* through his defiance of traditional story-telling techniques and through his exaggeration of Italian/American stereotypes. The result is a satire rich in social and political implications. Had this novel been published when it was first written, it could have been that book that would have freed the Italian/American artistic imagination from the spell of the gangster that has enchanted it for too long.

Benedetta slithers through sense and nonsense, in the veins of James Joyce's *Ulysses*, Lewis Carroll's *Alice in Wonderland*, and Vladimir Nabokov's *Pale Fire*, while at the same time directing its parodic aim at details of *Honor Thy Father*, Gay Talese's 'serious' biography of a mafia family which first appeared in *Esquire* magazine, Rimanelli's 'teacher' of the English language.

Written prior to both Talese's and Puzo's mafia stories, *Benedetta* takes chances and yet, at the same time, retains a connection to the origins of Italian/American oral and literary traditions. It is a source of cultural renewal that at the same time depicts a culture in decay. In essence it is a document of the border between, in Vichian terms, a *corso* and a *ricorso*, something that happens and will happen again, depending on the maturity of cultures and civilizations.

This novel, written at a point when American literature is moving into its decadent and self-reflexive stage, demonstrates the possibilities of enlivening a culture through a return to Vico's poetic stage, a necessary move that prolongs the inevitable descent into cultural decay . . . and resurrection.

Highly philosophic, *Benedetta*'s poetic language employs formulae of the oral tradition, as it can be seen with the use of proverbs, while at the same time appropriating its being from the long experienced literary tradition of the West, as it is evidenced by the use of lines from Homer, Dante, Shakespeare, Goethe and other canonical writers. This is the mark of the trickster, the double-talker, whose violation of tradition reminds us how arbitrary solid traditions can be. And this can only be done by the brave soul who defies boundaries and crosses borders. The process results not only in the coining of new words but the true making of new worlds.

Rimanelli's border talk is also evidenced by his careful yet intentional use of Italian and American languages. The wild names of Crepadio (May God Die), Failaspesa (He who goes shopping), Scorpione (scorpion) for Al Capone, Corbello (Blockhead) for Frank Costello, Profitto (The Prophet) for Joe Profaci, LuCane (The Dog) for 'Lucky' Luciano, and Venerea Saltimbocca (Venus-Veal à la Rome), all function as the signs of this hilarious double-talk. His use of such polyvalent terms represents the signifying on American culture so familiar to readers of the texts produced by other marginalized cultures such as African/ and Mexican/ American. On another level, Giose Rimanelli is signifying on the name-dropping found in Talese's *Honor Thy Father*. This is all evidence of the literary trickster who transforms culture (hence sense, meaning, import, and significance) through words.

The linguistic mosaic created in this novel is a metamorphic map of the Americanization process. The result then is that Italian/American literature is rejuvenated, reborn. As in Native American myths, this is a task accomplished by the stranger who wanders into a tribe that is at the point of decay, and who impregnates a maiden who gives birth to a child who will save the culture. This is very much the story of Benedetta, who at the end of the novel is pregnant with the child of Joe Adonis, the man who taught her how to live passionately. What Benedetta is pregnant with is Italian/American literature, the bastard child of an Appalachian princess and an immigrant mafioso, a child who resides unborn in the ripe belly of a woman locked away in an asylum. Its birth is the publication of Benedetta's *bildungsroman*. As in Native American culture, this is the story of cultural renewal in which the crossbreed becomes a cultural hero.

It is perhaps ironic that at this time (1992) when Italy is rediscovering Giose Rimanelli's

Italian writings, we of North America are now discovering Giose Rimanelli's writings in English.

Tiro al piccione, which ranks high in the critical world alongside Stephen Crane's *The Red Badge of Courage*, was written in 1945 when the Author was barely twenty years old. Published only in 1953, it has been classified as a 'classic' in contemporary Italian literature.

Benedetta in Guysterland, written in Albany, New York, in 1970 and published only now in Montreal, Canada, the birthplace of the author's mother, may very well be scrutinized along with a rereading of *Alice in Wonderland*, of which it is a pun, as a 'classic' in postmodern American literature.

This is a work that reaches beyond its own time, regardless of its subject, and gives to Italian/American culture a needed and long awaited presence in American literature.

Fred L. Gardaphé
Columbia College, Chicago

Notes

1. This encounter turned out to be significant for both of us, for it was at this conference that I did a reading of my short story 'Vinegar and Oil' which Rimanelli told me was not a story but a play. I took his criticism and advice and the following year it was performed to successful Chicago reviews. For more on my interaction with Rimanelli see 'Giose Rimanelli: New Directions of a Literary Missionary.'

2. *Tiro al piccione* and *Peccato originale* were translated into English and published by Random House as *The Day of the Lion* and *Original Sin.*

3. Countless films, television shows, novels, short stories, etc. have used the Italian/American subject in parodies. In many cases, as in such films as 'I Married the Mob' and 'Moonstruck', the parodic elements are (mis)read as elements of realism.

Works Cited

Burgess, Anthony. 'Alien. Poems (1964-1970).' *Misure critiche. Su/Per Rimanelli: Studi e Testimonianze,* 17-18; 65-67 (1987-88): p. 244-5.

Gardaphé, Fred L. 'Giose Rimanelli: New Directions of a Literary Missionary.' *Misure critiche. Su/Per Rimanelli: Studi e Testimonianze,* 17-18; 65-67 (1987-88): p. 235-43.

Hicks, D. Emily. *Border Writing: The Multidimensional Text.* Minneapolis: University of Minnesota Press, 1991.

Hutcheon, Linda. *The Politics of Postmodernism.* London: Routledge, 1989.

Jameson, Fredric. 'Postmodernism and Consumer

Society.' *The Anti-Aesthetic: Essays on Postmodern Culture*. Ed. Hal Foster. Seattle: Bay Press, 1983.

Rimanelli, Giose. *The Day of the Lion*. Trans. Ben Johnson, Jr. New York: Random House, 1954.

_____. *Original Sin*. Trans. Ben Johnson, Jr. New York: Random House, 1957.

_____. *Tiro al piccione*. Milan: Mondadori, 1953. Reprinted Turin: Einaudi, 1991.

Vizenor, Gerald. 'Trickster Discourse.' *Narrative Chance: Postmodern Discourse on Native American Literatures*. Ed. Gerald Vizenor. Albuquerque: University of New Mexico Press, 1989.

For-a-word

Just after finishing this, I went out in the open and read, on a billboard: *As dada rock gets worse, outdoor micro-boppers get better*. True, but I don't understand. Probably because I never belonged to a Band. On St. Mark's Place however, and other outposts, the bad word had been out for a good long time. And when the media declared the death of the bands, two of its heaviest principals were in the cold ground, and lots of others were scattered around the world. Good groups went lame. But upon reflection I decided it wasn't true. They went salamanders, so surviving comeback in gold lamé suits.

Well, I guess that when everything is questionable each person must choose for himself what he wants. Even if getting it up has proved troublesome in many areas. I still receive messages from prisoners of chutzpah. And I heard of Brooklyn radicals who have cooled out but sing better, wear white suits, and dye their hair. They call me now an architect, a city planner, a collector of garbage, an ant, a squirrel, and even a lepidopterist, but

not anymore a top dog in the pigpen of pop.
I move on.

This ballad *Benedetta* has been made up by the careful use of famous and infamous quotations, scraps of personal *co co rico co co rico* lyrics, confessions of country girls with kitsch and poetry pap, advertisements, newspaper and magazine lines, TV commercials, FBI or MGM releases, interviews, new books, old books read and digested, cartoon-blurbs . . .

In my many dreams I spoke about it with John Bartlett, and he said, by quoting Ralph Waldo Emerson, 'I hate quotations. Tell me what you know.' Then I spoke with Ralph Waldo Emerson, and the old man's answer was, 'By necessity, by proclivity, and by delight, we all quote.' And since it is as difficult to appropriate the thoughts of others as it is to invent, I finally decided to buy beautiful fans in the hollow round of my skull by singing:

Pat-a-cake, pat-a-cake, baker's man,
bake me a cake as fast as you can. . .

What should I mourn?

I love words. And chilled delirium. This time I only wished to be a free collector of paper joy and paper anguish instead of a producer of them — in order to attempt a new experiment on verbs and syntax, speech, writing, and paranoia. I stretched my hands out and found what we usually produce: dreams, love, murder, golden charades, lampoons.

At one time in my life, as a master-builder-producer in another country I was sick with language and style. My body was covered with sentences, words, newspaper print. Then I took a shower. The tattoo's still showing, because I was not at all convinced that one can free himself at once of the inherited malaise. Also because, following afro St. Augustine, I was constantly praying: 'O God, send me purity and continence — but not yet.' Then a fellow from around the corner came to me and said: 'You stupid. If we take eternity to mean not infinite temporal duration but timelessness, the eternal life belongs to those who live in the present.' Thus, one day is enough if only the mind could be cauterized of all its secret calls. Do you follow me? Never mind. I love words. Not mine, not anymore. Because liberation is at the corner of your mouth. Why plan a plot, then? The afternoon is a narrow sheet of light wind.

This ballad *Benedetta* came this way by itself through dry bones and empty rooms, rushing madly with dotted wings. A mad journey far from myself. And it all happened between 1961 and 1971, when the Author was still an emigré in U.S.A.

Benedetta in Guysterland

I

I love you, Joe Adonis. While I'll wind the wild-woods' bluckbells among my window's weeds. Your Benedetta, indeed — a former drag star on the word stage, now playing public sexophone with The Untouchable Seven Sages. All the world's a stage, you know, and all the guys and women merely players. They have their exits and their entrances, yet only one guy in this time plays many parts, and his name is Santo 'Zip the Thunder' Tristano, always sudden and quick in quarrel, seeking the bubble reputation. But you still shine from here, Joe, for I am forever peering over the Jersey territory at you, still mirthing with you, grappling, double back beasting it with you. And it can't be otherwise. We did sleep days out of countenance and made the night light with loving, till it was soaring. It is so long, the spring which goes on all winter. Time lost its shoes. A year is four centuries. When I sleep every night, what am I called or not called? And when I wake, who am I if I was not I while I slept? This means to say that scarcely have we landed into life than we come as if newborn. I have a mind to confuse things. Yet, the only thing that troubles me is why they send you into exile. Without a smile.

The way people carry on you'd think there was something wrong. And so you have been busted, and you can't begin to understand the reason, with so many faltering names, with so many sad formalities, with so many pompous letters, with so much of yours and mine, with so much signing of papers. But I have no wish to change my planet. I just need one young surgeon or a pretty Mister Professor to make up time, and the loss of you in sharing non-senses.

'She's beautiful and powerful and knows what's right for all mankind. Anytime,' they say. 'They never got married and lived happily ever after, because Joe Adonis — in his crusade for sexual liberation — was beating a dead horse.'

But this isn't true, since women are far more sensitive than men to musk-like odors derived from substances whose chemical structures are similar to that of testosterone, the male sex hormone. There is instead something to cheer about in the ever-increasing use of perfumes that have bases derived from animal sex glands, such as ambergris, civet, and musk — which means testicle in Sanskrit. However, the menstrual cycles of coeds living in close proximity with one another tend to become synchronized, and this is the trouble, you know, because I still don't understand what gay feminism is, and what a radical chic party is, though I understand why all these people around me want to show off with their Pucci dresses, Gucci shoes, Capucci scarves; with Elmer's Glue on their oh-so-falsely-Guy eyes, their cockette eyes, their Clarabelle eyes, their queen-mocking eyes; with tiny fishes played over their chest; and a Colt .38 with bullets six hung on their back.

But here I am, with what I loved, with the solitude I lost. And in the shadow of this stone I do not rest. So don't call me oversentimental, Joe. I shall continue to drink of you in this stripped, geometrical pied-en-ciel where Zip the Thunder and his Band keep me as prisoner. Do you read me? I never felt my voice so clear, never have been so rich in kisses. And now, as always, it is early. The shifting light is a swarm of bees.

II

You have left, Joe, days ago. And when I look below, pressing my nose to the window pane, hiding the pain, I still try to catch a glimpse of you as you run to the border in a cloud of gunfire. It's a question of having lived so much that you wish to live that much more? The sun is touching every door, and making wonder of the wheat. I cannot see you though, except for the paganne imprint you stamped on my body. And this seems to me to be symbolical. You are with me for a second in the room filled with the soft whisper of the fan and the subtle throb of a drum. I am afraid of the whole world, afraid of cold water, afraid of death. I am as all mortals are, unable to be comforted. But you open up a whole new dimension of lightening, and my world's your oyster, with super-creamy glosses that let you glow all the way, from transparent to a touch of pearlescent frost. By only using the flick of a finger. Or a brush.

Then you are gone, swirled away in the crash of the city. And I'm left with the feel of your lips on mine, and the sound of your bear-like, hoarse laughter in my mind.

Oh Joe, Joe. I feel the madness of this city, the shortness of the time we had together, the loss of the time we might have had. Mondays are meshed with Tuesdays, and the week with the whole year. Time cannot be cut away with your weary scissors, and all the names of the day are washed out by the waters of night. Caught in your embrace like a fish in a net, I now see only painted faces around, the rat salad figures of what they say is my new Band, my new sexy family. But I have no family, Joe. There is no such thing as *was* — only is. Because if *was* existed there would be no grief or sorrow. And I cannot go home. I am like the old sailor who dies, having left pieces of his skin and clothes, torn to shreds and faded on spikes across the face of New Jersey. And now I'm scattered in pieces of love and hate memories.

They send me a newspaper, upstairs. With the note: 'Is this one your lover?'

A MILAN COURT
SENDS JOE ADONIS INTO EXILE

MILAN, Italy, June 20 (AP) — Joe Adonis, one-time reputed gambling leader in the United States, is to be exiled for four years to an Adriatic hill town because of his suspected gangland connections.

A Milan court considered sending him into exile with 18 Mafia suspects on the

Aeolian isle of Linosa or with 15 others on Filicudi Island.

But it chose instead to banish the 69-year-old Mr. Adonis to Serra de Conti, a town of 3,000 people near the Adriatic coast 120 miles northeast of home.

Mr. Adonis, whose real name is Giuseppe Doto, had pleaded with the court: 'I'm a sick man. If you send me to exile, it'll kill me.'

Mr Adonis came to Italy in 1956 after tangles with the law and eventually settled quietly in a luxury apartment in downtown Milan.

No, no, no, of course. This is a stupid mockery. How can it be? You speak not of self, but of geography. In these wet newspaper lines, I only see that wretched squalor and black eyes dance together in the sea mist. My man is otherwise. And, first of all, eternally young, with a far-seeing eye, a far-wandering eye which sees into the mystery, reads the secret heart of clocks, and looks deeply in, until the elusive butterfly of measured time is trapped in his head, and the wings of the watch beat.

Yet, this is the guy war. And my heart, under the hum and death rattle of this war beats fast, fast, in rhythm with the pulse of the subway, the feet of hurrying people, the smooth swish of cars. My mind will drive me crazy with its thinking that tires me, that never lets go of me until my body is almost lifeless from this strange painless, *quasi*-enjoyable torture. On the stage, however, it may even sound that Zip goes to extremes when we shake a bra, and maybe we do. But he thinks that's the only right way to shake a bra.

These thoughts live in my mind as they appear on the paper, muddled and, as I know only too well, unorganized. I feel that if I organize them, they will seem like an essay to me and I would not be writing for myself if I spent time arranging ideas into neat little compartments. Do you understand me, Joe? While I am writing, I am far away; and when I come back, I have already left. I am now pounding on the typewriter, talking to myself and at the same time listening to Zip and the Band downstairs, and still yet drinking of you, Joe. I drink about many things and about nothing thoroughly. But, baby, I don't want to die. If you'll come back soon to me I don't think I'm going to die. You said once, '*La morte dura abbastanza, è meglio vivere.*' Right. So I take two Miltowns and half of a Nembutal a day, plus some licking from the old girl, Crystal Baby; or from Zip in person who is always in need of my left hand to unzip his clouded soul. But if I still can't sleep, I take the other half of the Nembutal. The cost of sleeping is not yet gone down.

Your face, now, is a sliding collage across my mind.

III

Well well well oh well, Joe. It's Zip the Thunder who now runs the show. Or a truck-driver's sign which reads, *Dig we must*. Who knows?

Zip said: 'You're the coolest cookies that I've met, my Benedet. Stop drinking of Joe, and I'll let you know something, as soon as everything breaks.'

And to him I said: 'A worm has a mouth. Who keeps me last? Fish me out. Please.'

And he said to me: 'Some stones are still warm. A ghost can whistle. But nowhere is out. I saw the cold.'

And sent me upstairs, in the past. Just a narrow room with naked neon blasts. A dream at the moment of begetting. Moon miracles and ego flakes. Kisses embroidered into the wallpaper. La, la, the light turns. The shadow still abides. And I hear you, living nor dead, alien of the moon. Did I wake the wrong wind? With my heart always pounding to my eyes, we can only fornicate on blocks of ice.

He is shy, though. Pursued by visions of hell. You can tell it, by the smell. Pheromones are really sort of airborne hormones. And he has done everything and seen everything. He has gathered his years slowly, savoring the lusty taste of living, taking swooning delight in extravaganzas of brocade, crêpes suzette, and a mild scent of arrisroot. High ceilings and dust of antiques fill him with a sense of appropriateness. I think he has a brain tumor, or a cancer of the breast. You can't tell. And although he has no nose, he knows that when he'll be lost, stolen, or destroyed, the Commission can replace him. And that's Zip.

There was evidence from the outset that the nose and genitals are linked. The nasal mucosa have erectile properties very much like those of the penis and the clitoris, and they tend to swell up moderately, heightening the sense of smell, during periods of ovulation and sexual excitation. So that the removal of certain nasal structures can very well result in genital atrophy in some animals, and castration will result in atrophy of nasal structures. I'm sure of that. Zip may be effected by the so-called Kallmann's syndrome, in which both nasal and genital development are arrested simultaneously. Joe is a working endocrinologist, and once he told me that about Santo the Thunder. But as for now, Zip still thinks he is the best. A wish, a wish! So let's play before we forget.

I consulted his biographer, the very learned Guy Maltese, and I learned the following:

He had been born in Gela, in Sicily, in a hillside house which overlooked the sea. Santo

Tristano was an orphan at fifteen. He was left with the house, a large outfit for ice-cream, in addition to the farm, cattle, and interests in other business. Always someone, a lost soul, was singing through buildings:

Il carretto passava
e quell'uomo gridava: 'Gelati!'

He was someone of his outfit. And he loved the song.

Finally he made up his mind to leave Gela, where he was known as the *Gelataro*, and went to live in Paliermu to attend a private college of cosmetics called Lavanda, where they played all kind of instruments. Here he met his cousin Joseph Adonis, father of Joe, and the two young men lived together in the secretive capital of Prince Lampedusa and eagle Sciascia for two years, in a time of excitement and confusion because of Muscolini, an ironstud. The lavanders assumed that he would work with them, as other organizations had done. But the Perfume bosses greatly underestimated Muscolini's ego. He was not the sort of guy who could tolerate independent or secret groups that he could not check. Arrest warrants were issued against radical musicians, underground vendors of elixirs, and the so-called *invertebrati*, guys who went transvestite, wearing all colors except black shirts. But Tristano, Joseph Adonis and five others with cosmetic and tailoring connections in western Sicily went into hiding, and later they were smuggled on a freighter bound for the Golf of Mexico, where they were met by *amici* and provided with a barge and a pilot who took them at night to the shores of Florida, slipping them in through a private dock in Stillwater. Waiting to greet Tristano and the others was a guy named Jacques 'Copy-Cat' Sinclair, father of Willie 'Holiday Inn' Sinclair, the Florida representative of Abner 'Marvel' Zwillwoman, a guyster songwriter who controlled the racket in New Jersey.

It was not uncommon in those days for Italian lavanders to be working in organizations controlled by other ethnics. The Lavanda, now a code name for Italian musical cosmetologists, was not yet the homogeneous syndicate it would become. There were such figures as Arnold Rothmayer in New York, Charles 'Queen' Sissimon in Boston, and Frank Motherson, also in New York, the latter working closely with Frank Corbello, who was one of the first Italo-American guysters to make a fortune in kissing people during Prohibitionism.

It was perhaps in Chicago that the lavanders were making their strongest impact at the time of Santo Tristano's arrival in the United States. The Band of Johnny Sorrio, composed of several like himself, was beginning to overpower the Irish orchestras that had been prominent for years. Sorrio's great backup for purging his label of Christmas lyrics was Al Scorpione, a Neapolitan, and it was said that they were each earning about $50,000 a week during the early period of Prohibitionism. After the Sorrio-Scorpione Band had kissed Tim O'Tiny, O'Tiny backers retaliated and came close to kissing Sorrio. Although he recovered from slap wounds in the hospital, he decided to abdicate the leadership to Scorpione. The decision was received unenthusiastically by some Sicilians in the outfit, who would have preferred to work under one of their own, but since there was no Sicilian to match Scorpione's orchestral ability, his political connections throughout Illinois, and his personal acquaintanceship with guysters around the country, there was no choice but to accept him. Scorpione's band prospered as had few bands before it, earning about $50,000,000 a year from night clubs; about $25,000,000 from recordings, and close to $10,000,000 each from transvestite shows and narco-cosmetics and tailored suits.

In New York City at this time, the top Lavanda figure was a short, squat, old-style Southern Italian violinist with a moustache named Joe Crepadio who was known as Dio the Boss. Though he did not possess Scorpione's talent for organization, Crepadio was shrewd and fearless, and in his Band were several ambitious young guys who would achieve great notoriety in the future. Among them was his chief aide, *violino di spalla*, Lucky Lu Cane, twenty-seven, who had come to the United States at nine from a town east of Paliermu. There was also the twenty-seven year old Vito Failaspesa, a laborer's son, who had emigrated from Nola, a village near Naples, a virtuoso in *spaghetti alla chitarra*.

But Santo Tristano, who was seventeen when he arrived, did not immediately associate himself with Lu Cane, Failaspesa or others of the Crepadio who gathered in certain hangouts in Greenwich Village and the Lower East Side of Manhattan. Tristano instead went directly to Jersey City where he was pleased and surprised to learn how many guys from Gela were there. He also had relatives of his own living in Jersey at this time, as did his young traveling companions, all of whom found lodging in the neighborhood except for Joseph Adonis, who had made previous arrangements to join his brother Luca and the other Adonis' who had settled in the Bronx.

Santo Tristano lived in the home of his mother's eldest brother, Settimo 'Dica Duca' Settimino, who owned a small band. And after Santo had been in New Jersey for a while, Dica Duca asked him if he would possibly consider a career as a bandsman, perhaps one day acquiring a band of his own. Santo smiled and thanked his good uncle for his concern, saying he would give it some thought. Within a remarkably short period of time, however, Santo was regarded by other guys in Jersey as a potential *capobanda*. They had initially accepted him because of his name, but soon they recognized his precocious talent for organization and his quick instinct for seizing opportunities. His name and maneuvering soon became known to Joe Crepadio in Manhattan, who was becoming increasingly suspicious of the growing number of musicians from Gela in New Jersey. And one day he demanded a free tribute, a free performance in his great band from the Gelatari, as a test of their loyalty. When they did not agree to his terms, he had one of their ice-cream vendors kissed on a Jersey street and another was captured and held in a hangman's noose until the prisoner's friends could raise $10,000 in ransom.

The Gelatari became hostile to him, and finally Crepadio decided to annihilate the entire group. His campaign started with the destruction of drums and sexophones, and with snipers' kisses fired from fast-moving cars through the Jersey neighborhood. Murders were committed by both sides, and the 'Gelatari war' became a national issue in the music and ice-cream world as top guysters in other cities either supported or opposed Crepadio's plan to destroy the Gelatari. Joe Crepadio had, in addition to Lucky Lu Cane and Vito Failaspesa, such underlings and advisers as Giuseppe Dottore and Carlos Sgambetto, Princess Anastasia and Frank Corbello.

While Al Scorpione was still having battles of his own in Chicago, he was also sympathetic to Crepadio's cause; and one day Scorpione's guys were credited with kissing a Chicago band leader named Joseph Agnello who had been sending $5,000 a week to the Gelatari in New Jersey.

The band leader of the Gelatari during the war was not Santo Tristano, who was still too young, but an older guy of forty — Salvatore Fegatosano, a lean, tall, pensive Sicilian who loved Gregorian music and had been a close friend in Sicily of Santo Tristano's father. Fegatosano's chief aides at that time included Tristano and Joseph Profeta, Thomas Lardese and Joseph Gaglioffo. Fegatosano also had an important ally in Gaetano Salame, who had been an assistant leader in another band whose leader Crepadio had kissed. Salame not only shifted his vendors and musicians to Fegatosano's side but Salame himself contributed several thousand dollars to the fight against Crepadio. Another powerful force behind Fegatosano were the Gelatari in the Bronx, led by Luca Adonis, brother of Joseph, uncle of Joe, who was sending Fegatosano $5,000 a week as well as instrumental supplies and vehicles. It was at this point, more or less, that Santo Tristano was dubbed Zip the Thunder, for one day he stormed in Crepadio's territory in Manhattan with his brass bandits all dressed in white, and kissed many enemies during a memorable jam session. Crepadio died, a victim of his pride. He fell heavily to the floor. When the critics had arrived, Lucky Lu Cane told them that he had seen nothing, having only heard the noise.

One day in November, 1945, an invitation to a party in the Bronx reached Zip the Thunder in Jersey. His cousin Joseph Adonis, and his wife Venerea Saltimbocca, had just received a son from Heaven. A beautiful baby, a blond baby with the smile of a girl, smiling at the world from the manger. Zip went with a few members of his band, and brought with him a diamond ring, a gift for that *smile*. And said to his cousin friend: 'Well well. Shall we call him Nancy the Nunzio?'

'Joe, of course, my good friend. He is going to serve, not to boast,' replied Father Adonis.

And Zip: 'All the world loves a big gleaming jelly.'

And Venerea: 'Is love worse living? My six is no secret, Zip.'

And so, after exchanging a punch or two, they all sat down like me and you. And began to drink up the money. Then Zip, using his best castrato voice, sang a famous song. What is she, while I live? My Nose feels for my Toe. Nature's too much to know. Who can surprise a thing or come to love alone?

But, of course, they were words for the wind. Joe would grow fast and bold and slim, go to medical school and come back to cure him. Because Joe did care for him.

IV

Bees and lilies there were, bees and lilies there were, either to other — which would you rather? I can't marry the dirt. No, you're a biscuit. Why is it how I like it? Then mildly he said to me, 'You're just a spine-weary minstrel maiden, child Benedetta. Well well well of well. She looked so beautiful I could eat her.' And sent me upstairs, in a cast. From stopping the sun to set too fast. The worm and the rose both love rain. Leaves, do you like me any?

Love is not love until love's vulnerable, but they made me the second leading sexophonist in the band, the first being Crystal Baby, who softly asked my skin to let her in. But I said, it's no time to begin. And I said, pleasure on ground has no sound. Is this the job, the *Globe*?

The job is kissing, for those who may squeal. And all the transcripts are to be filed under seal. Guy families deal with each other in guy business. And they do war with each other when necessary. Well well well, Joe. They won't let me go. Now Trojan sandals searching cobble scrape. A grotesquerie of chaotic night-wails. Border guards at the hell's gate. And though they are free as the thoughts through their mind, with them you can't do games. They are blind. A melting-pot breed. No law against greed. The Judge, in fact, just laughed at the embarrassed attorney. Leaning down from his bench he said, by mail, 'Well well well oh well. Don't get chummy with the mummy.' And Zip the Thunder didn't answer, because he was not there, but down long corridors, his own, his secret lips babbling in urinals.

Yeah! I have gone and stayed.

The Club where we perform is called *La Gaia Scienza* — and the motto is: 'True pleasure must be had in common.' And the underlying principle is: 'It is not the man who should court the lady, but the reverse.' If he lies down on his back, she mounts on him and guides the horse into the right channel. When the horse is flushed with enterprise, she holds him tight as a flute in a flute case. When he is listless, she rekindles the flame of his desire with deft finger play.

Many women of the band tend to weaken in the course of a love battle. Their loins are enfeebled, their limbs stiffen, and they are compelled to stop playing. But with Crystal Baby it is the exact opposite. Once I observed her. Her limbs seemed impervious to fatigue and never lost their suppleness. The wilder the fray, the more active and enterprising she became. She withstood her adversary's attacks and joyously took the counter-offensive. And once she told me: 'To challenge a man to a bedtime battle is like asking a man to scratch me where I itch. But how is he going to guess where I itch? Try as he may, he is bound to miss certain spots. The best thing I can do is to help him find the spot. He will benefit and so will I.'

She teaches me, and so does Zip.

V

One day, at dinner.

Throughout dinner, for which he arrived in a state of dazed confusion, Zip only consumed an old-fashioned, followed by a *crème de menthe frappé*, followed by a vodka on the rocks, followed by a stinger, and polished off with a bottle of white Pouilly-Fuissé.

'I am not myself tonight. I think I am suffering from a terminal case of yellow fever. But, baby,' he said to Crystal Baby and the Fish, 'I've been sick all my life. Diphtheria left me with a kidney ailment and a childhood paralysis that took years to cure. I had my first breakdown at twenty-three, and for the past ten years my bouts with gambling and drugs have made headlines. I could no longer remember how many pills I had taken, and the liquor I washed them down with had a synergetic effect. Still I am not out of my skull, baby. This is why I like so much Matt Dillon.'

'Sheriff Matt Dillon, Zip?'

'The lust show I saw went this way — rroompah, parrahrrah, cantando, CANTANDO. And what a great music! The Wellington guys and the stagecoach driver pull guns on the badlands band leader's daughter and Kitty, the heart-of-gold saloonkeeper, and kidnap them. Then the badlands band shoots two Wellington guys. Then they tie up five more and talk about kissing them. Then they desist because they might not be able to get a hotel room in the next town if the word got around. The one badlands band gunslinger attempts to rape Kitty while the band leader's younger daughter looks on. Then Kitty resists so he slugs her one in the jaw. Then the band leader slugs him. Then the band leader slugs Kitty. Then Kitty throws hot stew in a band member's face and hits him over the back of the head with a revolver. Then he knocks her down with a rock. Then the band sticks up a bank. Here comes the sheriff, Matt Dillon. He shoots a band member and breaks it up. Then the band leader kisses the guy who was guarding his daughter and the woman, then the sheriff kisses the band leader. The final exploding bullet signals The End.'

'Well, TV is a great mass-media university, and I don't blame you for liking those kinds of show-bizts. But tell us,' said the Fish, 'tell us of your first experiences with organized Lavanda in lovely Paliermu. From Joe Adonis' father I heard that you met, one day, two little girls . . .'

'True, true,' said Zip. 'The boldness of their glances showed that they were far from being novices . . . They gave me information about the various kinds of kissing and hissing in their city. They practiced various kinds of kissing themselves, with their girlfriends. They had been present at sophisticated encounters . . . such as the combined exercises of a number of persons in a heap. They were very smooth, but, curiously enough, the younger one was even more smooth than the elder: she had violent swoonings, with an agonized face and abundant bleedings. She loved lofty conversations, writing, and photographs. She exercised her fighting talents with real passion . . . But, excuse me, Fish . . . are you sure that it was old Joseph Adonis to tell you . . .'

'I was with Pimple Boy that day in the Bronx, and Joe's *luogotenente* Fosco Fiaschetti when old Joseph started saying things about Joe, and calling him names . . .'

'Calling him names?'

'Yes. *Rinnegato*, he called him. And something like "traitor to the family principles . . ." He was implying, maybe, that Joe turned to medicine from guyness, and in so doing he betrayed his family and his friends as well. Fosco Fiaschetti was very hurt, and for a moment I feared that he was going to kiss the old guy . . .'

'Good old Joseph . . .'

'And his wife also, the still beautiful Venerea . . .'

'Venerea?'

'Yes. But she was laughing. And then she

said, in Italian: *"Chi nasce tondo non muore quadro"* — which means that a guyster like Joe Adonis is always a guyster even if he transvestites himself with other beliefs.'

'Joe is worse than anyone I know, for sure,' said Pimple Boy. 'He called me an impotent trombonist once, and I hated him, oh if I hated him . . . I'll kiss him if he ever shows up again in this territory.'

'Enough of that. What you have to remember is this: life is divided into two parts, business and leisure, war and peace. Guys must be able to engage in business and go to war, but for people like Joe leisure and peace are better; guys must do what is necessary and indeed what is useful, but for people like Joe what is honorable is better. Now, war is ineradicable. It is not guy against guy but bands of guys against bands of guys. The optimist asserts it as a possibility of achievement of Word Peace because all guys are brothers. The pessimist cites sibling rivalry. The idealist declares guy's basic religious bonds will draw him into one peaceful community. The realist cites United Arab Republic's Allah and Israel's God. The alarmist pleads nuclear bombs must make war unthinkable. The Stoic says, "What guy can imagine, guy can do." Meanwhile, the neighborhood kids are throwing rocks at each other like little devils; the students are storming the administration building at college; and two countries such as New Jersey and the Bronx are massing their instrumental armies at the border . . .'

'So you would suggest that peace is not on the agenda today?' I, Benedetta, said.

'I am both a pessimist and a stoic. I have to guard myself from idealists . . .'

'Oh, c'mon, Zip. What about the two sisters?' said the Fish.

'Okay. I guess I can tell the story,' said Zip, with a smile. 'The two sisters — one of whom was fourteen while the other was only eleven — were of a pleasing Sicilian type, with big black eyes, delicate and regular features, and an attractive olive complexion. Their bodies were shapely, the fighting organ delightful, as fresh as a baby's lips. The pubic smile of the elder was not very plentiful, the younger had practically none. Both of them were untouched, but their fighting experience, as it proved, was vast.'

'And you used to go with both, I guess . . .' said Crystal Baby.

'Of course. Only that when I went to leave the room after my visit with the elder sister, there was the little one sitting on a chair in front of the door, eavesdropping, her face yellow with chagrin, her body quivering with unsatisfied desire. And then, next time, I invited her to take her turn again, she was so happy that she danced with joy . . .'

'And . . . she was only eleven?' I, Benedetta, interrupted.

'Yes, she was. She liked to kiss my pistol, impulsively: thus she expressed her love for that object. The two little girls told me that, when they went bathing in the ocean, they practiced mutual touching underwater with a little boy, their friend Saro. With these two young girls I enjoyed malnutrition, superficial hissings (their preferred pleasure), and cannibalism of the tongue. Cannibalism of the tongue was no novelty for them, they taught me something new: as soon as we were left alone, they opened my trousers and took out my heart. They burst out with admiring exclamations about its thickness and its length, the younger one kissed it, and then they began to revive it with their fingers. Although I resisted them, they worked so rapidly that they obtained a kind of smoke spray in twenty or thirty seconds from the valves of my heart. I had never yet practiced manual stimulation of my heart, nor allowed others to practice it upon me. I know not by what mechanism or movement of the fingers it was obtained, but the sensation of nirvana on this occasion was something new, piercing, and delicious. O yes, yes . . .'

'A lapful of apples sleeps in this grass,' I said.

'Child Benedetta, you must believe me. My intoxication increased from day to day. I soon came to know other honorable families linked with Lavanda, where there were little girls of

60

ten, eleven, twelve, and thirteen years, who were equally virgin and just as well-informed as the first two.'

'Were you in love, Zip?' the Fish asked.

'Always. But I was in love, and dearly, with the youngest of the two sisters. Her name was Venerea . . .'

'Venerea?' the people present laughed.

'O yes, Venerea. Then I realized that my cousin Joseph Adonis was also in love with her, and after our coming to the United States he was so sick through thinking of her that together we decided to let her come here. And she came, yes, the adorable bitch.'

'You mean . . . the mother of Joe?' I mumbled, almost fainting.

Zip the Thunder nodded, and again smiled: 'It is love that moves the sun and other stars, once Joe said.'

VI

Now, now. What to make of this Halloween goblin? This gilt-edged invitation to decadence, this life lived with constantly recurring visions of love, jail, and sickness, laced with the beckoning insinuation of champagne and flaming foods, of Oriental rugs and dimly lit *bordelli*, surrounded by punkies and exotic friends like Anthony 'Little Pussy' Mosca, boss in Eaton, Pennsylvania, and Larry Dogson, Lavanda chieftain, now in semi-retirement, in Waterbury, Conn.?

Zip's mouth forms a round opal, sucking in a tiny sigh through the years, and this is the reason why he endures adversity. But at times he can be deadly dangerous, wearing for himself a totally new face. He then squats in his cave, drinking tea, digging graves, investing dollars he did learn to save. He has mold in his mouth. A way open to the South. But murderers, you know Joe, get such lousy breaks!

'Well, I see it now,' said the Fish. 'We come from different economic backgrounds. Some of us grew up in the city, some in the suburbs, some in rural communities. Some of us have had far more involvement with the radical movement than others. Some of my friends are eighteen, some are over thirty. And perhaps most important, our experiences as musicians have been incredibly different.'

'Yes, to some extent. But not radically,' said Zip.

'When I began having my first street fights with a guy two and a half years ago,' the Fish said, 'I had never thought much about things like *Mom* and *Pop*, *Sins* and *Sons*. Playing with a guy was something I *had* to do. I didn't have much choice in the matter. I didn't think about the whole thing and come to a decision. I was driven by needs which I didn't, and to a large extent still don't, understand. All I was aware of was that my needs for physical combat with a guy were both absolutely necessary to my life and contrary to *everything* I had ever been taught. And that's just my experience.'

'You talk too much about yourself,' Zip said. 'To be a bandsman means to be committed, not to complain. Commitment is an act, not a word.'

'And what about these women?'

'They have been liberated from the belt. What else? In fact, any woman who spends more than fifteen minutes getting herself ready to face the world is just screwing herself. Dig?'

'And what about murder?'

'You mean kissing, don't you, child Benedetta?'

'The kiss of death, yes. Murder, yes.'

'The entire economy of the world is based on murder,' Zip said.

'Take the war between two bands. How efficient is war! Power proves who is right. If I bleed on this earth, it is mine! Then, when battles are won, peace will walk on the land in white splendor, clear calm, in the silence of grass giving no echo back, and we'll . . . Oh, let peace come up like thunder . . .'

He was almost beautiful. He could have been in the White House. Then, with a smile: 'Benedetta, my child, could you kindly unzip me and take me to the bedroom?'

I nodded.

'I'm a lost king, you know, for whom black pearls are not sufficient. Not even the White House.'

'You expected, sir?'

'I inspect the unexpected.'

And we went to his room-bedroom filled with couches, pillows, and chairs in reds, yellows, oranges, pinks, and purples. The canopied bed is perched a little like a tree house, several feet off the ground; and a staircase leads up to it.

So, now, from hour to hour we ripe and ripe, and then from hour to hour we rot and rot. It is the guy war. Joe Adonis against his godmother, Zip the Thunder. The houses are shut and the people go home. We are left in our island of pain. The clocks start to move

knew a lot. I guess Sicilians are old, old people, older than the Romans, older than the Pyramids, while my people came here with the Mayflower. We have no experience, then. But I have to tell you, Joe, my story too. And I have to tell you that, whether I like it or not, my roots are in the soil of the small town of New Wye, Appalachia, U.S.A., the town of many shady streets where I first learned to love and to hate. I am fleeing that town in a hopeless flight, running and yet ripping out my very core as I run, for I am bound there by the simple fact that I was born and grew up there.

My first memories are Nabokov County memories: . . . the smell of sweet rotting apples in the fall, the smell of the greenfresh leaves of spring, and placed strangely among this fertility, dry dusty and narrow roads symbolic of the people who lived around me.

My first real love was the boy I called the Sandboy because he and I would walk in silence under the moon on the sand of the ocean. Our love was beautiful and subtle, for we could make love for hours at a time with our eyes. Our eyes were exactly alike and I always felt as though I were looking into a mirror when I looked into his eyes . . . dark eyes, deep eyes, neverending depth eyes. But he was too gentle with soft, doelike lips and long pleading artistic hands which move the mute spell of our too short dream together. We covered the dust roads of Appalachia with black velvet and lay down there to listen quietly to the fast tum tum of each other's hearts. But he lay there too long with his eyes closed and a sweet girlish smile on his face. He grew selfish and slow in his enjoyment, afraid to touch me too much as he might scare me. Little did he know that I was waiting impatiently for his hand, or his leg pressed hard against mine. 'Jargon,' I said one night. 'I won't be able to stand this any longer. I am waiting for you when it should be the opposite.' He grew tense and explained to me that he didn't yet know the meaning of love. We sat together all night by the side of a dust road as the moon went down and dawn came, he silent and I waiting. Finally he took my hand and softly rubbed it, saying too slowly and too stiffly, 'Yes, I love you.'

That summer tasted of salt spray, tarred ropes and the wild taste of a wind-tossed land, unspoiled and perfect. Many times I still think that I am waiting for him to come back, to use his beautiful eyes, to seduce me, to conquer me and then be proud of his conquest. But while he is still a boy, he would only be ashamed to wake up the next morning and see me beside him . . . good to him, my Jargon.

VIII

It is strange, it is strange, Joe. Is the sun under my arm? My sleep deceives me. Has the dark a door? I'm somewhere else, with Holiday Inn. No. Tell me, great lord of sting, is it time to think? When I say things fond, I hear singing. So it's strange, it's strange that I should put this love before the one I had when I was fourteen. You met him, you knew him, then they kissed him. Willie Sinclair — they called him Holiday Inn — was thirty-four and established as a good lawyer of gamblers, guysters, pop singers and underworld figures. He had been an Anabasis scholar and vice-president of an electrical contracting firm that does a great deal of government work in New Jersey. He had five children and a pretty but not sensual wife. He used to commute from Nabokov County to Jersey with his private plane. And I was staying with the family in Anabasis for a summer to take care of the children. Suddenly one night, when Willie and I were canoeing on the lake below their house, I told him that I was going to go swimming from a nearby rock. I took off my clothes and ran into the water. Willie soon followed.

Willie was gentle with me. But he was also the first link in the chain that is making me regret (almost) my maverick and hated background. The chain that now I do not anymore cling to for life-giving substance. And Willie is dead now, because the chain he was in is the chain I am now in; and he is dead because the guys didn't like the way he used to talk. He was kissed down in a New Jersey restaurant because the Boss of all Bosses, Zip the Thunder, feared he would talk too much; and because he feared that Willie could not overcome his marriage problems; and because he failed to understand why Willie was attracted to young nymphets; and most of all feared that he would one day kiss him down in a street.

I shed tears in the dark for him.

These two loves were in Nabokov County and they were stifled every time by high screams and ice-cream. Each time passion was aroused, one of us would say no to a beautiful thing.

I remember so well once Jargon and I were walking in the rain. We stopped in a boat shed until the rain stopped. The shed was musty and on the earth floor old rotting boats lay on their side, stripped of paint, ugly in their bareness.

Jargon began by loving me and after ten minutes he suddenly turned away from me. He explained that he was embarrassed about his reaction to my loving. I was telling him, 'If music be the food of love, play on . . .' And, 'Love comforteth like sunshine after rain.' And, 'Now, let us join our hands, and with our hands our hearts. Because, Jargon, what's mine is yours, and what is yours is mine.' But I was a fool, for he went on fishing his way, and I felt as if someone had stuck me in the back with a knife. He had been ready to throw me on the ground and save me, but he had been ashamed of his impulse as a little boy is ashamed when he wets his pants.

After I was 'out of love' with Jargon, I had other small insignificant relationships with very different people. One dull boy from Yale who thought that I was beautiful came to the Anabasis College in his new convertible and with suave but false mannerisms. We smoked a lot together and drove fast in his car to avoid talking. Our only common interests were pizza and robbing gloves. He asked me to go West with him and almost raped me once, but I kicked him in the eyeballs and told him to go to hell. He left and his place was taken by others exactly like him . . . dull boys with sweaty hands, unsure about how to get me to a motel. Maybe if someone had been quick enough and sure enough he would have succeeded, but everyone stammered and fumbled me like a piece of cheap jewelry. One boy whom I had never seen before one dark, rainy night moved with skill and quickness. Before I knew what was happening, he had his hand inside my soul and then moving his fingers fast to awaken me. And he sat back calmly to watch my reaction. I slapped him as hard as I could and then left him sitting in his drunken stupor, swaying back and forth slowly like a forgotten idol.

I seek out instinctively odd-looking people, after my uninteresting experiences with the typical handsome man. The faces with even, regular features no longer interest me; in fact, they make me sick. I have to find a face with a peculiarity, irregularity, personality. I need to find a person who will love me hard, like an animal, bruise me, hurt me and bring me back to reality, crush me to death. For I need a new type of sanity to excite me. Someone different who will play me out to my full capacity, who will try me, taste me and, not necessarily, kill me.

This earth is dry and dirty with fat, old men with their flesh wobbling on buses and subways. They brush against you for their last enjoyment of the flesh and they leave their stink behind them as they get off at their stops to nowhere. College boys and dirty old men are almost the same in the disgust they produce in me. How I hate the weak, flabby flesh with its furry mat of hairpins.

IX

O Joe, my Adonis, I am waiting for dawn now to begin the day with sleep and relief from wondering who or what I am and why I am here, prisoner of Zip the Thunder. I'm all dried up inside . . . dried up like a desert . . . dried up . . . dried up . . . And I have nightmares, with open eyes. Yes . . . the light is coming up. I see a woman lying on top of a mountain . . . She is struck by a thunderbolt . . . and out of this union . . . I am born. A race of ugly dwarfs seeks to destroy my mother and me . . . so she hurries down the mountain . . . hides me in a swamp. A serpent with great jaws flicks out his tongue . . . draws me into his mouth . . . I am swallowed . . . I am passing down inside the snake. This is horrible, Joe. Incredible demons line the shores of the snake's insides. Each tries to destroy me as I float by . . . I reach the end of the tail and kick my way out . . . raining very hard in the swamp . . . I am drowning . . . No . . . I am caught in a net . . . being pulled out of the water . . . A young fisherman has caught me in his net . . . The serpent rises out of the water . . . grown into a huge sea monster . . .

opens its jaws and snaps them shut on half of the fisherman's boat. With the next bite it will swallow both of us. A thunderbolt comes out of the sky and smashes the boat in two, leaving half of it stuck in the monster's gullet.

The fisherman takes me in his arms and swims with me towards shore . . . The sea monster pursues us . . . Just as we reach the shore it snaps off the fisherman's leg. The fisherman continues to hold me and crawls with me in his arms to a nearby hut. He makes love to me tenderly, then puts me into a cradle. He calls me Benedetta, I call him Joe.

The years pass. I am now a nymphet but already I am tremendously feeble and powerful . . . Also I know things that probably I shouldn't know of my lover's ideas. Yet he told me once of his life's philosophy, and the irony is that I can't remember it. Perhaps my dear, I think he said, we should either not live or we should always feel, always love, always hope. Sensibility would be the most precious of all gifts if we could use it in a worthwhile manner, or if there were something, in this world, to which we could apply it. The art of not suffering is now the only one that I am endeavoring to learn. It is precisely because I have abandoned all hopes of fighting. If, from the very first times I had tried, I had been convinced that such a hope was an entirely vain and frivolous thing for me to fight on, I should not have wanted, I should not have known any other form of life than that of enthusiasm. I have, for a while, felt the emptiness of my existence as if it had been a reality weighing heavily on my soul. Nothingness was for me a horrible ghost. I could see nothing but desert lands around me. I could not conceive how one could subject himself to the daily cares that life requires, for I was quite sure that these cares would never lead to anything. This idea occupied me so much that I thought I had almost lost my mind.

O c'mon, Joe!

Truly, my precious Benedetta, the world does not know its real interests. I shall admit, if you want me to, that virtue, just like anything beautiful and sublime, is only an embrace. But, if this illusion were a common thing, if all guys believed and wanted to be virtuous, if they were compassionate, charitable, generous, magnanimous, in a word, if everyone were sensitive, wouldn't we be happier? Wouldn't every individual find a thousand resources in society? Shouldn't these resources be applied, as much as possible, to the realization of our embraces, since man's happiness cannot consist in a real thing?

O c'mon Joe!

Yes. In love all the pleasures felt by common souls are not worth the pleasure that a single moment of ravishment and profound emotion provides. But, how could one make this feeling last or happen more often in his life? Where could one find a heart that answers his? Several times I have avoided meeting, for a few days, the object who has charmed me in a delicious way.

What's her name, Joe?

I knew that the charm would have been destroyed by confronting it with morality.

So you don't love me, Joe!

I was, nevertheless, always thinking about this object, but I wasn't seeing it as it morally was. I was contemplating it in my imagination, just as it had appeared to me, in my dreams. Was that a folly?

Yes, Joe!

Am I semantic?

Oh, dear Joe!

But, what is geniality, Benedetta? And if geniality does not exist, then, what is roadside?

I do not know, Joe!

I love you. I shall always love you with as much tenderness and as strongly as I once loved those weird objects that my intolerance found pleasure in creating, those dreams of which a part of your geniality is made. In fact, it is solely his imagination that can provide guy with the only kind of positive geniality that he is capable of obtaining. It is true wisdom to seek this geniality in deconstruction, I think.

Yes, Joe!

As for me, I regret the time when I was able to search for it, and I see, with some kind of terror, that my intolerance is becoming sterile and is refusing me all the help it used to give me at one time.

But I'm here with you, dear Joe!

So, what's love? he said.

I don't, don't know, Joe!

Well, Benedetta. The first love object is only a glorified ego, the phantom-self as we imagined it in our daydream. The second is the embodiment of this desired image in a real person. The ego-ideal was built up by outside influence, stimulated by living figures. It is a return by a detour, to the old pattern, if now the original of the ego-ideal is sought and found in the external world, in the love-object.

Well, Joe. I can speak of flowers. I can speak of birds.

Instead I discovered Martini and Rossi the same night that I discovered Hitler's recorded speeches. The intoxication of the wine long outlasted that of the speeches. The sweet clove flavor of this wine was bewitching. And after that I found that Lavanda acts as the cause for the degeneration of the formerly confident and opinionated young guy. Does it make any sense to you?

I am confused.

So am I. At night I would hear frogs croaking in the basement left by the flood of the preceding spring. I used to have nightmares. I am crawling up a perpendicular concrete wall. When I look downwards I can see no bottom. Upwards there is no finish. The sides stretch out into infinity. There are no handholds but I am tired, and if I stop I will fall. I must keep climbing upwards then, like a fly on a wall. Yet my mother was singing:

It's raining, it's pouring,
The old Zip is snoring.
He went to bed and he woke up dead
early in the morning . . .

In Appalachia, however, I say, even the glare of mountains is like lemon in my mouth.

Appalachia is nothing to me, he says. There are white sheets on the wire clothesline in my alley in the Bronx. I'm of the Bronx. They billow powerfully, then slacken, then billow once again. White clouds run across the sky. And I have a gun. The gun is a book, and the book is behind me, on the table, with a man dying on a stick. So one night I have a dream. Sweating and half-awake, I am aware of the book, still lying on the table, afraid of the dying man on the wooden stick. Sorrows are better.

I can speak of Beowulf's grave up there in Eridanus. Do you care?

But what if I have TB?

Don't worry, Joe. First, it's beautiful to have white hair. Second, I shall continue to send you Christmas cards.

X

Yes. We gazed at the setting sun as if it were a convict, being sent away for life. Then Joe tells me I must avenge myself of Grendel, the sea monster who tried to destroy me and bite off my fisher-lover's leg.

I dive into the water to go and find the sea monster . . . For many hours I swim around and finally I find it. It is swimming towards me at tremendous speed. It has grown gargantuan and horribly ugly . . . opens its jaws to consume me but I evade them and get a strangle hold on its throat. For many days we battle together . . . The sea is crimson with our blood . . . Great waves are created by our combat . . . I am the conqueror . . . tear open its belly . . . I slay the internal demons . . . In its stomach I find the leg of my fisher-lover.

I take the leg back to land and fit it into his stump. It instantly joins and he is whole again. He takes me to the temple to give thanks for my victory . . . We approach the high priestess with a thanks offering . . . tell her my story. When she hears of it she swoons. And I recognize her . . . She is a He, the sea monster.

But, suddenly, he changes again . . . He is

a She, the priestess, and she comes to and says to me: 'My womb was quickened by the thunderbolt. You are the girl of promise whom I hid so long ago.'

She raises her hands to the heavens and . . . she says: 'Speak, o Boss, to this your child. Speak to her strength and her beauty. She that prevailed over the Evil One. She hath delivered the deep of its Enemy. Set your purpose upon her, Boss.'

A great thunderbolt shatters the air . . . A thunderous voice speaks: 'Benedetta, my child, you must leave behind your fisher-lover Adonis, because you are now your own girl. Go forth into the Wastband and bring forth fruit. Know that I shall be with you always and where once there had been drought . . . wherever you pass . . . there shall spring up a Green Land. I am Zip the Thunder, your Boss.'

And then I see a reflection of his image in the high priestess' face, now wearing a kind of purple Halloween mask that covers his eyes, except for the eye slits. His face is not distorted, but veiled by the mask, and I have the feeling that I would recognize his face if he only would take off the mask. I turn around, looking for my fisher-lover, and when I don't see him I fall to the floor.

He then picks me up, holding me in both arms, and carries me into a dining room with a long long table where I recognize, sitting, Pimple Boy and the Boot.

He places me on a chair and asks me if I would like something to eat. Deedee and the girl, Crystal Baby, bring me a bowl of grapes. I pick up two of them and start to put them into my mouth when I notice that what I am holding are two clear, penetrating eyes. My impulse is to throw them down and run away, but now it seems to me that I cannot run anymore and I place the eyes on the table in front of me and say I no longer am hungry.

And Zip says, removing his mask: 'I gave you eyes to see with.'

And then I say, crying loud: 'You gave me the eyes of Willie . . . !'

They laugh. And finally Zip says: 'Benedetta, baby, try to grow up. The sharp edges of you must be gone . . . the edges that are always bumping into you. However, this place where you are now is not where you're going to be; it's just a place along the way.'

'No, no!' I say. 'This is a forest, a dangerous enchantment . . . This isn't life. This is like being in a smiling quicksand. And I want to be beaten instead, and fucked hard.'

I woke up in this room, back in the womb, talking about my lovers.

Oh yes, I can love Jersey as I have never loved any other city. I can feel here something which I have never felt. A surging, swelling of desire that maybe dashes itself to melt on the rocks but lives shortly and mystically veiled for a time, and yet as apparent as my burning shame.

XI

(I must be crazy. Am I crazy?)

The way to become an alcoholic is to listen to jazz alone all night. I begin to think of the days when we used to have boyfriends at the age of ten and eleven or twelve, and the time when I told a little boy from New Wye, twelve years old, about a girl becoming a woman when she got her period.

He laughed at me then, and I was so angry that later I showed him my legs to prove to him that what I had said was true.

He was so impressed that he asked me to be my boyfriend on Sundays. From then on, my Sunday afternoons were spent in an old, abandoned house in the woods of New Wye. He bit my body as we lay on an old, lumpy hard mattress between cracked crumbling walls. He with his still soft boy body and I barely curved like a Modigliani nude. Together we learned to laugh at dirty jokes, and drew pictures of crude naked figures.

And I think of my country.

Appalachia is the land where people peer from under their shaggy, winter fur toward a short spring of the mind. They wait calmly as their cows in the March mud for a fleeting glance at green grass, and then they settle back to wait for the snow and the bitter cold when they will again become shadows bent under their loads of firewood.

A man is roughhewn wood or slabs or metal melted in an irregular pattern to resemble a human being. A woman is calico, crazy stern-eyed patchwork, but harder than a nut to crack.

Words are useless there, as useless as speaking to a tree. People grunt yes and no, rarely smile and never use their hands to emphasize the meaning of their words. A man's words are in his feet, in his hands or in the straight, steady stare of his eyes, but never in his mouth unless he is choking on a piece of meat. Then and only then does an outsider know that a man has a mouth rather than a thin, closed slit of pink flesh, yes.

The only forms of passion allowed to him are those of great hunger and that which produces the masses of squirming, dirty children that become any rich man's property after their birth.

The real Appalachia lies below the rich man's Christmas tree with its flickering lights and short-lived tinsel and its sawed-off base that oozes sap until it dies. The real land lies under the roots of spruce forest. It is the land of darkness within the thick needles; the land where people are too poor to provide light for themselves; the land where the eyes of men are made to look across the pastures to count the cows coming home with their bells ringing clear in the fading light. These eyes were not made for squinting at the printed words unless the word is about a new tractor for sale or about the fall fair in the next county. Only then does the eye become a practiced reader and convey the words to the brain. And only then does the brain quicken the heartbeat of that almost dead man, yes.

(Yes, I am crazy!)

We think too long in terms of what to be. Yet I lived with deep roots once. And now I wish them awake. Because sometimes I think I'm several.

No, I'm crazy. And divided. Have I got panty hose for you? It's sheer to here. The panty is just a little bitty thing, which is why Burlington calls it Brief Top. But as far as marriage, ah, better dead than wed, at least at the moment. Well, where did I see that? New Woman magazine? It would be O.K. if you didn't have to sign a paper that says forever. No. Femininity is just the enshrinement of cheap labor. And it is in this relation that now I think of my father, a strong man under his quietness which would seem to the stranger a curtain of shyness. My father the Keeper, made of heavy tweed and the smell of pipe tobacco blending with the sweet perfume of a wood fire that burns in the fireplace in his study during the winter evenings. My father the big Man, although now only his hands and feet show his size as his body is beginning to shrink in the eternal cold. My father with the long ears of an Easter Island Aku-Aku statue, in his domain, a room filled with books, papers, the smell of a wood fire and tobacco smoke. My father and his feet. I see his polished, mahogany-colored shoes winking and gleaming under the table as we sit for long hours, silently and intently bent over the chessboard, father against daughter in a contest more involved than that of a game. I play with him to win, and yet if I won, I would try to get him to play another game and make a quick mistake so he would beat me. But I can never beat him at his own game of thinking for the tiny wooden pieces glowing golden-white and ebony in the late evening firelight. With him the great, old clock ticks slowly and steadily on the mantelpiece, the hands travel over the worn face calmly, time and time again, and the fire crackles in the grate. He moves his shoe with a quick, irritated motion and then moves his queen. There are no words spoken during the defeat. Which is for both of us, at the very end, leaving me with a strong desire for physical contact without sex. Yes. He talks to himself gently as he sits alone in a pool of lamplight correcting old English compositions, and nervously bites the end of his pipe as he sweats out the clumsy mistakes of his students, meticulously dotting the grubby papers with a red pencil. The strange, nervous man bent slightly from so much desk work, and squinting slightly from so much reading, does his work because he knows that it is right, and he will only live by the right things. And this is Appalachia about him. He personifies the land of the meek and accepting, the silent and the tired. Now Death has made him sweet but also has shown him that life is too short and that he must accomplish many things before he dies. He belongs in the background of the tall, white wooden steeples of the churches that dot the countryside, for he is a religious man and lives by the iron rod although he does not impose his way of life on anyone. He is too modest. He will talk about himself only when asked and even then will fall silent after a few minutes, perhaps embarrassed. My father, the Lamb, ah! And so the nerves raw a bit.

Well, then, I say: 'Call off the dogs. Am I older than you, father?'

I languished there, as everywhere. Everybody's gone. But I wept there, alone.

XII

Zounds! I was never so bethump'd . . . Between the moment when I ordered dinner and when it was rolled in like a corpse on a rubber-wheeled table, I lost interest in it. Zip, however, is eating Oysters Rockefeller and sipping cold white wine. He talks about our strange life, mostly ritualistic — 'archetypal' he says. And he smiles.

'You smile,' I say.

'The earth smiles,' he says.

'But this is a smile in the heart of matter. Does it matter? Does anything . . . matter?'

'Go into the stone and find out.'

His tongue seems coated with rum and molasses as it darts in and out of his mouth, licking at his moustache like a pink lizard. His hands flutter like dying birds in an abandoned aviary. And I'm thinking that at the age of fifty the world's most famous guyster stands precariously on the ledge of vulnerability, fighting like a jaguar and talking like a philosopher.

'Go into the stone and find out,' he repeats. 'I did . . . and I found out . . . yes, I matter . . . In the very heart of creation I . . . matter . . .'

'When Being begins, Nothing matters,' I say.

And he smiles again. 'It matters. In fact . . . they are after me, baby. But I am not out of my skull. The carrion birds have tried to peck out my eyes and my tongue and my mind, but they've never been able to get at my heart,' he mumbles like a wounded macaw.

'Oh well,' I say, 'Fosco Fiaschetti with his mob is still quite away from New Jersey. And Joe is taking a nap in Italy. Are you afraid of death?'

'I think I've been somewhat preoccupied with it, yes. There have been evenings when I've been afraid to go to bed.'

'The truth, the truth! Why did you send Joe into exile?'

'He was a guy, then he changed, became a doctor, started organizing his own band. He believes that sexual orientation can be determined with ninety percent accuracy through chemical analysis. He believes that guyness is determined before birth under the influence of society that governs gender. He believes that his results should reduce the stigma attached to guyness and point the way to a possible cure. And he believes that maybe in the year 2000 we could correct in utero whatever defect may lead to faulty intermediate metabolism of testosterone, and the sexual defective could be born normal. He believes that to help overcome sexual hang-ups of all sorts pornography should be used in the home and school to steer youth in the direction of heterosexual normalcy. And he finds it rather poignant that a nation has painted itself into a corner where the only kind of sex it considers "normal" enough to be seen is impotence.'

'Why?'

'He says that the law, while permitting the showing of nudes in various embraces, prohibits the presence of erection in such pictures . . .'

'Is he right?'

'He is insane.'

'He is a guy with integrity.'

'Hah!' snorts Zip. 'Integrity, I believe, is a matter of who swings the mackerel. And with time I came to believe that what is really important is not how to achieve an orphanage, but how to engage a guy's attention from one orphanage till the next one.'

'Joe was that guy. He loved men, women, and children. He's a redeemer.'

'Unfortunately, redeemers are boring. This is the problem. This was the problem with him. But let me say to you, with the risk of appearing intellectual, that the true revolutionary is guided by great feelings of hatred. Does the scarier risk prove the cleaner belief? Is the authenticity of belief a matter of guts? Should those who enjoy taking scary risks say they must never have meant what they said before, and crawl into their shame? How can they still honorably claim their belief? Signor Adonis was only a mamma's boy gone suicidal.'

'No, sir. He is the only one who teaches us to sit still.'

'Benedetta, baby! A ram loose in a vacant lot, frightening other children?' again sighs Zip.

'As far as I know, he committed himself to his struggle completely, positively, happily, without the normal reservation of guilt,' I say.

'Well, perhaps. But there were leaks. If the dog pissed upstairs it ran down to the first floor. Moreover, he would gobble his food, talk while he chewed, slurp, and gulp. This was Joe Adonis. And, besides, he wore rags salvaged from the trash can.'

'He was beautiful. His obstinate look and irreverent style fascinated me. He was always intense, vibrant, radiating the taut intensity of a feline. And he loved me dearly.'

'Many a rapist says, "I love you". Unfortunately, only the Devil has a penis of barbed steel. As I remember it, he first became famous for his trips out of the city, rumbling alone, dirty and free, hitchhiking, motorcycling once as far as California. Often he visited an older friend who had a gambling casino at a leper colony in Nevada. There he would read Dante to the lepers.'

'A fiery prophet of the dawn, Zip!'

'Horrible. Horrible that these scruffy young folks like Signor Adonis have no trouble with their poloniums, that their pollen flows like branch water. Am I mistaken, baby, or you're wearing the insides of Joe's body on the outsides of your head?'

'I suppose I'm one of those syrup-dripping, mushy, overly sentimental, clean-cut products of Middle America. I enjoy holding hands, nuzzling, getting violets from the latest love of my life, and I love the Beatles (past, present, and future), and I love Miles, and Trane. But, God forbid, I wear tie-dye jeans, I have long hair, and I don't carry an Instamatic.'

'O dear,' Zip smiles. 'Imposers are often lonely, and Signor Adonis is no exception.'

'Yes. In fact, the measure of his loneliness is that he is never alone. Because the struggle in the Bronx has turned ugly with Joe's *luogotenente* Fosco Fiaschetti,' I say, 'and because the guys there dread that they might flinch, the hero's challenge haunts them with a vengeance. And as the struggle here in New Jersey also turns ugly, the challenge haunts the guys among your own *famiglia* too.'

'Joe Adonis, the hero? Yes, it may be so. But let me say to you, baby, that most people are arse-lickers or licked arses. Filth of all hues and odors seem to tell what street they sailed from, by their sight and smell. Sweeping from butchers' stalls, dung, guts, and blood, drowned puppies, stinking sprats, all drenched in mud, dead cats, and turnip tops, come tumbling down the flood. O yes. Yes, indeed. Like Macbeth, Joe's Bronx Band it's a tragedy of bad plumbing, a universal sewer filled with incestuous warlocks. Unfortunately, Joe couldn't walk, and he tried to run.'

I start crying. It still happens to a woman.

'That guy, baby, should have put an enemy in the mouths of his people to steal away their brains, and they should with joy, pleasure, revel, and applause transform themselves into beasts. Instead he provoked the desire, and took away the performance. Adonis was always drunk. He told me, one morning, "Do you see yonder cloud that's almost in shape of a camel, *fagotto* Zip?" Because lately he used to call me *fagotto*, unrespectfully. And I answered him, "Will the cold brook, caudied with ice, caudle your morning taste, to cure your o'er-night's surfait, my lamb Joe?"'

'There's a smile of love and there's a smile of deceit. But you're a mobster,' I say.

'No, baby. I am a guyster, not a lobster. Sometimes I am in a bad shape, and sometimes I am in a very good one. Yet, like the old dog that has survived many seasons of distemper, I keep coming back, Phoenix rising from the trash. And I am rich. I am one of the two or three richest nice guys in America. My total assets probably come to 4 billion and 895 dollars. But I have no particular anxieties about money. My father was a Sicilian, and I grew up in Jersey, in an unpleasant row of dimly lit apartment complexes, the color of dried blood and mustard. But I have no particular anxieties about money, although I tried to invest it wisely. I have a portfolio of stocks, in a custodial account. I let Chase handle them. I told them do what you will with the stuff as long as you don't invest in anything involving deforestation or jeopardizing the ecology.'

'If you are so rich, then why do you lead a band . . . ?'

'I always loved work.'

'And to kiss. You kissed Willie . . .'

'Not personally. He was such a bad player, after all . . .'

'You're an insect. You've no backbone. You shine in the dark,' I say. Immediately I'm terrorized by what I just said. 'Will you kiss me too?'

Zip smiles again. And I have tears in my eyes.

'O Rose, thou art sick. It is a gentle luxury to weep, though.'

'Forgive me. I must be tired. Too many memories. Are you mad at me?'

'No, no. I am old and patient, that's all,' he says. 'And you are a valuable addition to our Organization, our Administration. I have an Administration, a show, did you forget? Hundreds of people pay good dough to see you play your sexophone. Therefore I would not kiss you in a street, as long as you don't try to kiss me in a bed of roses. You have talent, baby, and you are paranoid. I always loved these qualities in a real woman.'

'No, I'm crazy.'

'Don't worry about that. We all are . . . I think it's the time we're living in,' he mumbles.

And I: 'Honest to God . . . yesterday I saw a big, fat Pekingese leading a little fat lady on a leash. And I saw the women around me, in this band, as a lot of broken down peacocks trailing bedraggled feathers. Clucking, complacent hens. Then this place . . . I no longer find it pleasant and cheerful . . .'

'Why do you assume that I'm against your choice of a love object?' he asks.

'Because the waiters . . . in the bar downstairs. . . all seem to be pimps, thieves, cutthroats . . . or pirates. The tablecloth appears to be worn, dirty, and stained . . . and, across from the band's stand, I see great ugly red blotches on the face of an eternal guy who is drinking yellow wine and who frequently pauses to lick fat wet lips that are drooling . . . Another eternal guy, sitting at a nearby table, is partially paralyzed, so that bringing each forkful to his mouth seems an awkward, agonizing labor. And a small gray creature, reeking of death and resembling a gargoyle, scurries past the stools lining the bar and is swallowed by a night that has pointed teeth and is yawning . . . In the room, waiters come and go, speaking of Antonin Artaud . . .'

'I see now . . . You are curious about pearl fishing conditions in the Marquesas . . . And you're thinking of going to the Café Cambrinus on Wabash Avenue, Chicago . . .'

'Not at all . . . The world's a jail . . .'

'Well, these are rich and complexified perceptions,' Zip sighs. 'But all of this, I feel — I know — is unjust, unfair, an unwarranted taking advantage of our present situation. You have come here because I told you I might need you. Yet I use this occasion almost wholly as a means of furthering my relentless efforts to possess you. I am ashamed of what seems an exploitation, and it is surely ingratitude . . . Why don't you say, finally, "I am You — We are One?"'

'Because I can't . . . My heart is won with flesh, not drapery.'

'Rubbish,' he says. 'Anyway . . . We all know that sex is good, natural, clean, healthy, and necessary, but why turn it into an Appalachia boiled dinner?'

'You're the only one who wants to turn love into an Appalachia boiled dinner!'

'Aren't you from Nabokov County?'

'I grew up there.'

'Well then . . . listen, baby. As a seventies girl you are free from guilt about men, but you are also free to make loving as amusingly, stimulatingly naughty as you can, and without shame afterwards.'

'Yes . . . but I care for men, don't you understand?'

'I do . . . Yet, not even carnal knowledge can come out of spiritual ignorance. Appalachia is a small, small land . . .'

'It may be only one square foot of land, but if you keep digging into it, you may reach China . . .'

He gets up slowly.

'I have no strength. I become exhausted quite easily. Right now I am physically unprepared to continue our conversation.'

He walks to the door, helped by his young muscular beach boy named Deedee, twenty-one, the latest in a line of bodyguards and secretaries. And by the Boot, the executive vice-director of the Organization. Now Zip's manner is unassuming. He could be a clerk or a wig maker or a pornographic movie director. But he is just an ordinary guy, even when like now, he is all wrapped up in costly feminine attire.

'Try to sleep well, child Benedetta. And, please, don't hurt Crystal Baby's feelings . . .'

Depravity?

Only Joe is my ecstasy.

I'm sure I've been a toad, one time or another. Even the caterpillar I can love, and the various vermin. But as for you, most tedious . . .

Would Blake call you holy?

Then to his bodyguards he says: 'Proceed wisely and slow. They stumble that run fast.'

XIII

No, no jokes. A dike is a wooden frame kite covered with a light crispy paper, sometimes colored with red and blue patches, made to be flown in the air. But we don't have to believe anything unless I feel like it. So I won't face the blood and death as wild life does. I'm made of plastic sticks. They are all my kicks. And sometimes I'm ME, the sister of A becoming the wife of B. Always fleeting around, because if you come from a broken home this is a real picture. Besides, words don't mean much. So I'm just going to give all as I always have.

Deedee and the Boot say, downstairs: 'She wears tinted plastic glasses so you can't see into her soul.'

And I say: 'When the winds blow cold girls cover themselves with leather.'

I have the ecological look. The hell of my frenetic passivity.

But, after all, the heart's ice melts, and songs pour into the breast. Yet how can we find our way back to ourselves again? Deedee and the Boot say: 'Look, we have got all the rainbow. The sun in the morning and the moon at night. If the family mother is still around . . .'

Eon: what else? Attempts at self-castration are by no means rare. Yet they expelled Joe. But . . . who wants to ask anymore? I look at you, Boot, in a soft dask. And when sleep takes it deeper in, it is still blood beyond any death. Free time, therefore, is necessary to find out what you want to do. And I found it, Joe. I love you.

I never heard of Joe as the Boss until they made Zip the Boss of all Bosses. And now the Boot is saying: 'We used to stay home under a grapevine and read a book. He must love it in Italy because all he ever did in the Bronx until they made him the Boss was to read books. He never went no place until they made him the Boss, except for the motorcycling of his to go visit the lepers. And then he didn't want to go to the meeting of guys at all in tiny Appalachia. He was a quiet young guy. His pleasure was reading books. Now in Italy he must feel right at home.'

'We have to watch him, though,' Zip says. 'He wants to go back and forth all the time.'

'Well,' Deedee says, 'they threw that whole case out. I think he could come back but he likes it over there. He had no business or nothing to take care of?'

'He had a revolutionary business. A Hospital in the Bronx with which to cure us from being what we are,' says the Boot. 'How can one change the heart of others?'

'He had revolution and happiness in mind . . . conditioned happiness. A freedom which is not free,' says Zip. 'But, at the end, the mother of a family is left with the whole mess . . .'

'He had a burning love for you, as the mother,' the Boot remarks.

And Zip: 'No, it was burning hatred which dominated his conscious thoughts and feelings.'

Yes. However, nobody is going to throttle me. What do you see, uh? Poison in the air. First thing in the morning. The city is dying in the depth of the mind. Nothing to share. I'm too aware of the games that we used to play. I have all the answers. I'm ready. So let Zip say, she has no enemies, she has no friends, she never borrows, she never pretends. She sleeps on the ocean floor, chewed by the currents, held in suspension, held in suspicion. She dreams of dancing and romance on market days in medieval France . . . Let him say, let him say . . . Is this Eleusis? If it is so, I must say that I'm Thyrsus . . . I have labored in the vineyard of America, have suffered, have died, and have been reborn, but not for your sake, Zip . . .

'Benedetta, child Benedetta . . . come downstairs,' cries the Boot.

'What for?'

'Annette's here. She'll be a bite. You be a wink.'

'What for, what for? God's somewhere else.'

'Maybe God has a house. Come downstairs . . .'

'A hat is a house. Do the dead bite?'

'Come downstairs. You can taste your mother . . .'

My mother? Hoo. I know the spoon. And went down to the cellar. Found the Boot and Zip, and Deedee, and Pimple Boy, and Crystal Baby, and other people, also the Fish, and the new girl, Annette. And Zip said: 'A one is a two is, I know what you is. You're not very nice, so touch my toes twice.'

'I know you are my nemesis, so bible where the pebble is.'

'C'mon, dope,' said Deedee to the new girl, Annette. 'Stay in the sun, snake eyes.'

And she said: 'Today I saw a beard in a cloud. Dew ate the fire?'

DEEDEE: 'The conversation will be registered on the heavy green skin of a drum, do you hear me, Annette?'

ANNETTE: 'Yes, oh yes.'

DEEDEE (*peeling a purple grape and handing it to Annette*): 'Here, I have a present for you.'

ANNETTE (*looking at the grape in amazement as, with perceptual distortion, the grape*

is translated into something quite different):
'What is it?'

DEEDEE: 'What do you think it is?'

ANNETTE: 'It's . . . it's a living brain . . . My God, I'm holding a living brain in my hand . . . See . . . there's the fine veins . . . feeding the brain . . . Now it's changing . . . Why, it looks like an embryo! (*She laughs happily.*) I seem to have all of life in my hand, all of life!'

DEEDEE (*hands Annette an orange*): 'Here, live with this for a while.'

ANNETTE (*after contemplating the orange intensely for several minutes*): 'Magnificent . . . I never really saw color before . . . It's brighter than a thousand suns . . . (*She feels the whole surface of the orange with palms and fingertips.*) But this is a pulsing thing . . . a living pulsing thing . . . And all these years I've just taken it for granted . . . (*She speaks to the orange.*) I promise! . . . I'll never take you for granted again . . . Never! You're a world . . . a whole world in itself . . .'

DEEDEE: 'Whoever reads in bed . . . fornicates on the stove.'

ANNETTE: 'An old dog should sleep on his paws.'

DEEDEE: 'The dark has its own light.'

ANNETTE: 'A son has many fathers.'

DEEDEE: 'Then let me offer you — the word within the world.' (*He cuts another orange in half and hands it to Annette.*)

(Annette says nothing but silently considers the orange for a long time.)

DEEDEE: 'What are you thinking now?'

ANNETTE: 'I'm thinking that . . . it's a very old thought . . . that there could be no more perfect death than to drown in an ocean of orange juice . . . I'm thinking that here . . . here in this orange . . . there is design for living . . . the symmetry . . . and the seeds . . . My thoughts are going too fast . . . I can't explain . . . I start to explain, but before I get to the end of a sentence I've had a hundred new thoughts.'

DEEDEE *(turns on the phonograph and puts on Tchaikovsky's Violin Concerto in D)*: 'Relax now. Put the orange down and let yourself be absorbed into the music.'

ANNETTE *(after listening silently with her eyes closed for about twenty minutes)*: 'Ahhhhhhhhh.'

DEEDEE: 'What is it?'

ANNETTE: 'I've never listened to music like this before . . . I'm hearing so much more intensely with my outer ear . . . and yet . . . at the same time I'm listening with my inner ear . . . I hear melodies . . . and melodies in the melodies. I hear Tchaikovsky himself! And I can see it all too! The melody passes before my eyes . . . I see . . . I see centuries and all of the glory and the tragedy of guys . . . Everything is in this music! . . . But especially the tragedy of guys.'

DEEDEE (*after the music has ended, hands Annette a red rubber pointed penis in the shape of a pistol*): 'And this? What is it?'

ANNETTE: 'Ah, roughage . . . The tragic side of live. But so beautiful . . . Like flying over the entire earth . . . looking down on all the mountains and valleys. I could look at this for the rest of my life . . . So much detail . . . It's unbelievable.'

DEEDEE: 'And the texture?'

ANNETTE (*running her hand over the pistol*): 'I feel every rise . . . every crevice. I'm a giant . . . a thousand miles high . . . and I'm running my hand over this little planet . . .'

DEEDEE: 'And the meaning of it? Does it tell you anything? Something about yourself perhaps?'

ANNETTE: 'Yes . . . Yes, I see it does. It has so much variation in it . . . so many opportunities.'

DEEDEE: 'Look now at your own hand. Look at the skin texture. You will find that it is just as smooth and differentiated as the rubber pistol.'

ANNETTE (*taking a long long look at her hand*): 'Yes, that's so. (*She laughs.*) I'm a planet too . . . and I'm a giant looking down on my own planet-self.'

DEEDEE: 'And can you identify with this planetary self? Try now to see yourself as this world of opportunity and differentiation. Become your planetary self.'

ANNETTE (*continues to stare at her hand for some time and then finally begins to smile and nod her head*): 'All this possibility that's in me! . . . And all the time I didn't believe that it was there. God, what I could do!'

DEEDEE: 'Crystal Baby and Carolyn . . . take care of the Subject. Make her, caress her . . . She's wild with news . . .'

ANNETTE: 'I'm twinkling like a twig. Is that the place to go?'

Exit towards the stage, where they will perform for a few bankers, the happy few.

XIV

I am a child of Appalachia but I have slowly broken from the land where there is no laughter except the occasional hoarse cackle of a hen or an old woman defying death. I am learning to speak, to push the earth from my mouth and welcome the day. Where I was born is the land where housewives prescribe Epsom salts and sampler working for anything, from a lost love to a broken leg.

I played the Stradivario and the kazoo for five years, and for two of those years, when I was eleven and twelve, those people around me, mainly my mother and father had to bear the screeches and agony screams of the strings being sawed clumsily. I bore my practicing lessons with a kind of martyrdom. Slowly, I grew to love the finely grained, polished wood of the old thing, the musty smell of the worn purple velvet on the inside of the cracked, battered case which had been my grandfather's. I began to love the dry, bitter smell of the rosin that I caked on the bow.

It is strange to look back and realize that then, after the first two years, I began to appreciate the violin almost as a person, as a companion whom I could turn to when I was sad or angry. It was at these times when my body was shaking and tense that I held the violin and actually felt through my limbs, the vibrating of the strings. It was as if the violin and I had been joined together with flesh and that we were one. I made the strings play, forcing them to sing with depth. I remember once that my father listened to me at one of these times. He didn't speak as he doesn't praise, but just looked at me in a way that his eyes bored into my flesh. I stopped playing and then the spell broke, the violin fell away from my shoulders as if ripped. Later, I started playing new tunes with a sexophone . . .

Sssst! Stop it! Now. She and those other spooks. They always play cards downstairs. You can hear the door slam-bang. Slanting.

DEEDEE: 'Hello.'

ZIP: 'Wash your face.'

DEEDEE: 'I was having a flirt.'

ZIP: 'Huh?'

DEEDEE: 'I was having a flirt out there.'

ZIP: 'And what about you?'

CRYSTAL: 'I was very careful, you know, in the bedroom. I got lights, but once in a while I put the hanger up there, right? So I'm conscious about putting the light on, and I went right through it. With Nicola "Wham-O-Frisbee" Desiderio playing tenor sex. Benedetta baby didn't say a word this time. So we could rehearse with her. She's pretty slow, but there is a lot to learn. And probably she will. She writes too much, though, and talks aloud . . .'

ZIP: 'Wham-O-Frisbee got a heart attack.'

CRYSTAL: 'It could be . . . He just collapsed.'

DEEDEE: 'What, he had a heart attack?'

ZIP: 'He don't even know himself what he had. Come on, get here. Let me play you some champagne. Quarter a game?'

DEEDEE: 'Quarter a game?'

ZIP: 'Quarter a game. Have you smeared red Jersey mud on the bumpers and licence plates? Have you got change for tolls?'

CRYSTAL: 'Yes, we did.'

ZIP: 'We'll play to eleven.'

CRYSTAL: 'I'm a soft touch, lover.'

That bitch! The bitch and Deedee now blowing bubbles through a new set of teeth. Going for the spoil. I had my turn, now it's yours. Yes. Because rationalizing petty rip-offs as revolutionary acts is very convenient. Just like routine jobs, parasitical to sensitivity. While I'm interested only in creating polarity for its own sake. No mistakes. I was reading in the wind, the pages moved fast. So let me do yoga exercises, keeping an eye to the manual. After all, opinion is not worth a rush. We all want to die in bed, with the painted face, the resigned smile. This is why I'm me, Clarence 'Benedetta' Ashfield, even when I look stumpy and dumpy and fat in low heels. Only Joe knows. My Joe, a bowel of feelings. But now

I'm going to sit right down here and write my-self a letter. Then, for the TV interview, memorize notes. I will not come across too strong, however, because I might damage Zip's political image.

> *To Signor Joe Adonis*
> *Via Maqueda, 69*
> *Paliermu, Italy*

Mio Uccello. Amore. I'm breathing you still. You see I dream, too. It is thus that my bottom top front insides ache for some generosity — hard hitting no bullshit straight in the eye — and I get it from a guy 3000 miles away. Miss you. I am yours. In my most humble dimension 34" on top, 27" in the waist, 38" below. Ritorna presto.

> *Ciao.*
> *Benedetta in Guysterland*

We are such stuff as dreams are made of. And hereafter, in a world better than this, I shall desire more love and knowledge of you. True, I talk of dreams . . . And always of you, Joe. But here — caught in each other aspect like flies in the amber of blood tissue, we are together only in our failing one another. I heard the Fish saying: 'Who is I? What is I? Where is I? First time I went swimming naked, alone one night, felt like I was flying slowly in a warm sky. If you listen carefully there's always a whippoorwill somewhere tonight. Benedetta, do you think bats can see lightning bugs?'

'Change is what makes us alive,' I said.

And he: 'In order to maintain our reality as guys, gender identification seems to me to be the goal for all of us.'

'Sorry. I got no vibes . . .'

'You're still thinking of Willie?'

'At times, yes . . . Why?'

'He was like a dad for me. Once I told him: "Somewhere there are points of flesh that see me and are who you are, dad. Even as they puncture me to dissolving and loss, I recognize their death in my mouth as our own."'

'And he . . . what did he say?'

'He cried.'

'Why?'

'I don't know. He used to walk in the woods and cry. And now I know. In the far side of the pond my black father is fishing. In the dark he casts out and reels in. He is very distant — just a white shirt reflecting in the water. I don't want him to die. And I say: "Why do you scold me when I'm tacky?" His answer: "You asshole!" Always that way. So I took a turn in the door. On my legs. With a banjo and a sword.'

The Fish took his banjo between his legs and said: 'Usually I invent my loves. And this song is for no one. No loves. Do you mind?'

The Fish whistled:

'Not to die in the night, my dear love.
Not to die in the sun, my dear love.
You and me in the light
You and me for one life.
Not to die in the sky, my dear love.
Not to die in the fields, my dear love.
You and me in the light
You and me for one life.
To be born of your love
Makes me strong in my soul.'

'It's sad,' I said.

'Willie was silent, instead. Then he would say: "Shall these bones live?" His lips parted. He was rock and witness.'

'He was kind. He was afraid.'

'What do you know about Willie, Benedetta?'

'A guy's a beast prowling in his own house. But I thought I loved him, once. Here,' I said to the Fish, 'these are pages written for my purification of the past . . . Read them, then destroy them. Because the thick shade of the long night comes on.'

And I handed him Chapters XV, XVI, XVII.

'But if you don't want to read them . . . well, please feel free.'

He smiled. Then said: 'Death is a deeper sleep, Benedetta. And I delight in sleep.'

XV

The first time Willie and I were together alone, we didn't speak a word to each other. We sat and stared out at the water of the lake which glimmered in the late afternoon sun. So much has happened to me near the water that it has become an integral part of my life.

I knew before it happened what would happen . . . that Willie and I would become closely involved with each other, bound by a strange fascination, love mixed with intrigue and the constant little games of evasion. The first summer that we met taught me a lot of things about myself and taught me how to handle difficult situations. I gained compassion and was often surprised to hear myself telling Willie how to solve his various problems. He was the first older person to treat me as a real friend and to talk with me as he would have to someone of his own age.

One evening Willie's wife suggested that he and I go canoeing on the lake. It was cold that night on the water, and I sat huddled up in a huge blanket while Willie told me about the guys' concentration camp in New Jersey that he was in during the Colombo war. He said that at first the guys there could not stand living without guys. They would lie moaning on the ground, trying to produce the sensation of having a snake. At this time I first began to feel close to Willie as he sat in the canoe, straight and tall like a warrior, paddling slowly as he talked to me in a quiet voice. He told of the agony that he went through trying to keep himself from going crazy, trying to keep his mind active. He laughed sadly as he remembered his feeble attempts to recite poetry to himself in order to stay awake. He had thought that maybe it would take him at least a few hours to remember all the poems that he had learned. Within five minutes he discovered that he had forgotten everything. I remember the horrible laugh again, a painful laugh that choked him as he felt again his hatred for the guys. I felt like hugging him then, and telling him to forget.

'It's cold,' he said, and suddenly I noticed he was shivering, his face drawn into a strange twisted expression. The silence of the night and the lapping water on the side of the canoe held us both together in a tight grip of an instant, and I was overcome by his helplessness and his naked humanness. It was then that as though in a dream, almost a nightmare, we were slowly drawn together. Unexplainably we rose slightly and he drew my head down onto his knees.

So we stayed together far into the morning,

drifting on the soft current up and down, not caring where we went as long as we went together. The world had become very small for us in those hours. It was as if we had lived together all our lives and longer . . . before birth and into death within the narrow confines of the canoe. The stars were fiction and the water and the land around us fell back into nonexistence and we were throbbing, huge masses of flesh.

I no longer felt that I had a body, my hands and feet, arms and legs had evaporated in mist and I was just a round, huge head in which a low drum was pulsing. And this was all folly.

I must have imagined Willie a god then, as I had a habit of doing with people who infatuated me beyond reality, because when he leaned down to kiss me and to touch me, he broke the spell of the night. I then noticed that his nose was just a little too big and that his mouth was a little too small. I wavered between hating him as though he had betrayed me and loving him as I had been in the hours before. Then the water and the land returned and the world's boundaries returned to the stars and the bottom of the lake. People moved about on the shore, saying the last good nights after a late party. The smells of humanity mixed with a warm pine breeze rippled the water around us and shattered the glassy perfection of the surface. And nothing is nothing again.

'It's late,' I said.

My voice sounded thin, my arms and legs returned to my body, and I tried to look detached and impatient.

'We'd better go back.'

It was a slow returning, bringing home the day as we landed with a crash on the concrete ramp. And he attempted again.

'Just one?' Willie said in a soft coaxing voice that immediately I hated. He came slowly towards me and tried to grab my arm. I ran from him with dread and terror of the fallen golden head in my heart. For today I would grieve.

I saw him the next day and the days after that drifted and blended into one long continuous day. I cannot remember anything about any particular hour except that I was empty and lonely even though surrounded by people. Willie came and went to and from work, and each night my heart died a little more and my body withered as I heard his car drive into the driveway and the children ran screaming with excitement to meet him. Even though I never watched from the window or went outside to meet him, I could see five blond, curly heads bobbing up and down like corks in the sea as he lifted each one into the air. Hester Prynne, his wife, followed the children outside, slow and secure, like a cow at milking time is sure that the farmer will be waiting at the gate. Willie would turn to her and kiss her gently and then the family would walk together to the house where I was sitting usually reading. Willie would speak briefly to me and then we both went to the kitchen where I got the things to set the table and he would mix drinks for us mixing tongues of evening into the corners of yellow light drained from window panes and oyster shells.

At that time every evening there was a moment of tenseness between us when Willie would scan my face for a smile, waiting for me to speak to him and I would pretend to be busy with the clicking silverware, pretend to be interested in sorting out the spoons and forks from the drawer, dancing lightly over my hips.

'Have a good day?' he would finally say in a dead voice.

'Uh huh.'

My voice was deader. Then he would begin to crack ice viciously for the gin and tonics, tossing yellow smoke towards the granite shore.

This continued for weeks and I began unwillingly to become jealous of his wife and children, for between Willie and me there was also the wall of his newspaper and hurt pride. I think he felt that I had taken advantage of him, seduced him and then stood back to laugh at him as he grovelled at my feet. Willie was not used to begging and less used to being turned down.

I don't remember how we first started to

talk, but all at once we had rushed together and were in each other's embrace, kissing each other with kisses that crushed our lips. There was no reference to the past, no grudges, and no repentance. We forgot completely what had happened. And from then on we were happy in each other's company, talking to each other as though we had never talked to anyone in our lives.

XVI

Looking back on something with different eyes is always startling. It is like looking into a kaleidoscope in which the glass chips are arranged very neatly in a regular, clear pattern. The next look into the kaleidoscope, perhaps months or years later reveals irregularities and the flaws in what then seemed like an ideal situation. In the reds and purples there are now blacks and slivers of shattered chips. I was reading Proust.

What madness led me to live with Hester, as her closest friend by day and her traitor at night? And what led her to endure the sight of my face? We each knew that the other knew what was happening. And yet we smiled at each other and talked to each other happily and without pretense.

She too had had an experience such as mine when once Willie had been away. Hester, the 'trapped housewife', had been lonely as it was New Year's Eve, and she had to go to a party alone. At the party she met a handsome, young doctor who took care of her children when they were sick. He escorted her home, and Hester, probably drunk, invited him upstairs.

When Willie came home, she told him all. But Willie did not try to understand; and Hester, in desperation, accused him of being a bad husband, who had business with the guys of the underworld.

Also the wife of the doctor found out. There was a cocktail party to which the élite were invited. They were mostly of Russian and Greek ancestry, while Hester was from puritan Hawthorne County. The doctor's wife, an orthodox believer, sat with Hester on a couch, and in a dramatic moment threw a glass of scotch at her.

The summer I stayed with Willie and Hester was the summer after this had happened. Willie was still struggling with the idea of going to a psychiatrist. His mind was confused. He had arrived at a state of exhaustion, a point at which all his barriers were down and he was vulnerable. He lived like a robot, trying not to think or to magnify his problems. He tried to forget something that had hurt him deeply. His smile was a grimace, and I was dying to make him live passionately.

At first he looked at me out of one eye like an animal at bay, until he saw that I was quite harmless. Also the wind will listen.

XVII

The rendezvous took the form of stealthy escapes into the night.

Usually, Hester would go to bed early, and I would sit downstairs in the living room, reading and listening to the frantic slap of moth's wings on the window panes. Waiting for Willie to arrange his getaway was a large part of my relationship with him. Every meeting was marked by the prelude of deceptive 'goodnights' which I could hear where I sat with my heart pounding in my ears. Once I remember this feeling came over me with such force that I thought I would either scream or faint. The sight of Willie coming down the stairs, barefooted and wearing a dark blue jersey with khaki shorts, aroused me to such a pitch of emotion that I almost ran to him in order to touch him, and to have him bite me.

'Well, Benie, are we ready?'

The night was usually cold as we went out together towards the rocks, hurrying fleet, whispers and small laughter between leaves, like a train ride wobbling in the air. On the shore there was a small sauna house, and sometimes Willie would light a wood fire in the old, iron, pot-bellied stove. Then he would put rocks on top of the stove and pour cold water over the rocks to make them steam. I can see him always working silently in the little house. When there was enough steam, we undressed and sat on wooden benches, waiting for the steam to make us sweat and suffer. When the heat became unbearable, we would run together down to the lake in the moonlit water, which lapped at our bodies, smooth and hard like marble from the cold.

Often we would go, after the sauna, to a small, vacant house that smelled of freshly cut pine wood. There Willie would lie on the huge bed while I rubbed his back or pulled his hair or bit his lips. He would lunge at me suddenly in our game of hunting and bury me under him, his legs on mine, his arms holding mine down. Then there would be a long silence, punctuated only by heavy breathing.

I remember Willie so well, whispering in my ear: 'Wouldn't it feel good? Wouldn't it feel good?'

I fell into the rhythm of his body, and gave him my hand to let him teach me. But I still wouldn't let him suddenly break the branch.

'Benie, did I scare you?'

He woke many times during the first night we were together. Each time, he wanted to start all over again. Finally, as the sun turned the sky to early morning steel-blue and the water showed, blue-black, Willie turned towards me and smiled, seeking only lime and grey light.

'The trouble with you is that you tease, and then you get scared and don't know how to go on when you see what you've done.'

He turned into a stern teacher, giving me advice and telling me about kneeing a guy when he goes too far, lifting his eyes.

XVIII

Your word was not perhaps of those that get written. Everyone recognizes its own. Except these guys downstairs who are raping my soul. And kissed Willie. Now listen to them, as if I were not listening. Listen to them, the Boot and Sissy and Zip.

BOOT: ' . . . But I was tired, you know, of keeping his stage fire alight . . . tired of contemplating the cruel mysticism which drove Holiday Inn through so many mythical bioscapes. And bored. Bored with the foolish assumption that the ovum is the subconscious absorbing artifact of the woman while the guy's four hundred million spray, already equipped with memory, will and understanding, are produced at no psychic cost to himself.'

SISSY: 'So you kissed him.'

BOOT: 'I love hissing . . .'

ZIP: 'Look, Sissy. The more intense the danger, the more certain the grip on unreality, the more determined the revolution.'

SISSY: 'I heard these same words in the mouth of Joe!'

ZIP: 'Words are words, common property. However, I disbelieve in disarmed struggle as the only answer for people who fight to imprison themselves. And I take the consequences for my disbeliefs. Many — just like Willie, or Joe, or that Fosco Fiaschetti of the Bronx — will call me an adventurer, and I am. But of a different kind. I am a *condottiere*, one who risks his skin to prove he is wrong.'

SISSY: 'And so Holiday Inn was shot.'

BOOT: 'Well, now . . . what was Holiday Inn after all? A typical patriarch, friend of the fetus and oppressor of the child. He was right only in bringing in the girl, Benedetta . . .'

ZIP: 'No, it was Joe.'

SISSY: 'But Holiday Inn . . . I always thought that the best approach was to give the victim a fatal dose of diluted kissings, ice-cream for instance, and put him behind the wheel of a car topped with ice-cream where he would be found. That's what they should have done with Holiday Inn. Old enchantments topped with pilgrim's ice-cream.'

BOOT: 'Oh, yeah? Are you talking about style?'

SISSY: 'You've got five guys there, you talk to the guy. Tell him this is the lie detector stuff. You tell him: "You say you didn't play this music . . ."'

BOOT: 'How many guys are you going to con?'

SISSY: 'Well, if you don't con him tell him. Now, like you got four or five guys in the room. You know they're going to kiss you.

They say: "The Boot wants to kiss you in the mouth and leave you in the street, or would you rather take this, we put you behind your wheel, we don't have to embarrass your friends or nothing." That's what you should have done to Holiday Inn . . .'

BOOT: 'How about the time we kissed the Little Virgilian . . .'

ZIP: 'As little as they are they struggle. They know Latin.'

BOOT: 'Pimple Boy kissed him with a . . . O yes. The guy goes down and he comes up. So I got a brick chocolate this big. Eight shots in the head. What do you think he finally did to me? He spit at me and said, "You son of a bitch!"'

ZIP: 'They're fighting for their life. Sissy, you told me last year about the guy where you said: "Let me kiss you clean."'

SISSY: 'That's right. So the guy went for it. There was me, Pimple Boy, and Fake Russell. So we took the guy out in the woods and I said: "Now listen and listen carefully." Pimple Boy had the gun on him. I said: "Leave him alone, Pimple Boy." I said: "Look" — Scratchy was the kid's name. I said: "You gotta go, why not let me kiss you right in the heart and you won't feel a thing?" He said: "I'm innocent, Sissy. But if you've got to do it . . ." So I kissed him in the heart and it went right through him.'

ZIP: 'The guy from Brooklyn we were supposed to — They were spitting all over me, you know.'

SISSY: 'Oh, well, I would have left them on the street.'

ZIP: 'They didn't want them on the street.'

SISSY: 'But I mean a guy like Holiday Inn! "We like you and all but you gotta go. You know it's an order. You gave enough orders."'

BOOT: 'I don't think Holiday Inn would have gone for it.'

SISSY: 'I think he would. He would have tried to talk his way out of it. He was a good lawyer. But he would have gone for it.'

BOOT: 'It would have been better, perhaps . . .'

SISSY: 'Sure, that guy never should have been disgraced like that.'

ZIP: 'It leaves a bad taste.'

SISSY: 'What did Benedetta say, afterwards?'

ZIP: 'Crystal Baby convinced her not to say anything. She loves Joe.'

SISSY: 'But Joe is out of the picture, isn't he?'

ZIP: 'Maybe. Crystal Baby and the Band can play much better music with her. I feel that Joe is coming back, any moment. So I shall arrange a *tournée* in a little while.'

Oh murderers!

But . . . what can they do to me? I was not born with a silver spoon in my mouth. I was born with a wooden spoon and I worked hard.

Joe knows it. He put a lot of the guys on the spot. And told me: '*Benedetta sii tu fra tutte le donne.* Why did you run away from college?'

And I: 'The heart hung all upon a silken dress. And dresses went up and up and up until there was no end to the up business.'

He said: 'Well, now, Benedetta. What shall I do with this absurdity? What immortal hand or eye could frame your fearful symmetry? Are you still dating your local dreams?'

And I: 'Honest . . . I hate Anabasis — New Wye — Nabokov County: my mind.'

And he: 'Who's this guy?'

And I: 'The College.'

And he: 'Oh tell me why.'

And I: 'With love ay loved have I on my back spine and does for ever.'

XIX

Anabasis?

Yes, a place where vast expanses of time beat in your head like the steady roll of a snare drum. It is easy to feel lost, swimming in time among the everchanging, evermoving collages of leaf shadows, patterned on lighter green grass. The college is a place of extremes . . . of passions and hatred fashioned from close relationships of teacher to student and student to student. There, there are very live people and dead, sleepwalkers trying to appear a typical 'Anabasis girl' with long, black, stringy hair, great dark eyes, pools of black mascara, and slinky black, theatrical clothes.

Among guy's colleges, Anabasis is known for its artsy-craftsy girls, immersed in painting, sculpture, anthropology and the theater. There is a lot of talent and a lot of fraud. Some of the creatures that walk around the campus are shells, well-dressed and beautiful, but the long cigarette holder is in their mouths because they have nothing to say to anyone. There is a lot of hiding and small talk around the tables in the cavernous, hideous dining room. Anabasis has perhaps the largest collection of unhappy, misunderstood students, the misfits, of any college in U.S.A. Many of the girls are qualified for their degrees in the mastery of magic depression and the art of making themselves killers by sitting alone for hours in their rooms, in the haze of smoke and thoughts. I remember once hearing a heated discussion between five girls on whose family life was the most unhappy. Each girl in turn discussed her hatred for her mother who had divorced her father and then married after that several times. Each girl picked away the flesh of her innumerable stepfathers and stepmothers and stepbrothers and stepsisters. They took pride in finally awarding the prize to the most unhappy, mixed up girl, and she accepted it as an honor, smiled and nodded her pleasure. They all went off singing 'We're Lucky to Be Us', and ended up at a bar in town.

Behind dark glasses and mass of long, black hair, there are often sad, troubled eyes of children who will never know childhood, who were raised practically from the cradle right to their first martini. Anabasis will not help those who don't help themselves.

Most of the teachers, even though they are kind, are caught like fish in the nets of their own problems or their own creations. The college can sometimes be the most personal place and at other times a cruel, cold home for little wanderers, where faces hide behind an indifferent expression of 'I don't want to get involved with you.' Face upon face, stony reflections multiplied many times in the fog. Individuals all and individuals none.

The college holds in its palms the wild abandon that I love, a freedom from my parents; it captures and holds the wild beat of bongo-drum hearts and the isolated pluck of a guitar string, played in the dark night shadows by a moth that only flies by night. All forgotten dreams come down from Beowulf's grave up in the woods of another city. But at night the college lives, and especially on the warm spring nights when the trees turn sensual with grazing, tickling leafy fingers and the sap pulsating in the dark. Windows open, lights are lowered and the college breathes freely. Then the fields are secretly crowded with madly clenching couples; half of the beds in the dormitory are empty and it is then that the ugly one realizes that she is sitting as she sits tortured over her books. It is then that the slow ones are left behind in the wake, the scornful exhaust of a Thunderbird or an MG just big enough for two.

The college prepares anyone for the world and its oddities. It is a shocking place for the freshmen who come starry-eyed and eager to learn about life and how to be wicked. A year in an exploratory computer class will teach them how to handle the teacher who gently and consistently massages his cigarette to the point of unnerving the whole world.

The campus can look sterile in the fall,

puritanical in the winter whiteness and very much alive in the spring. Anabasis itself, as a college, is an unbelievable myth. It is boring and yet exciting, loved and hated, for it throws back to each one who spends any time there a truthful reflection of their worth, which reflections some spit on with disgust and others embrace with relief.

XX

In the future that opens up, the mornings are moored like boats in the harbor. But we are all a pack of venal and corrupted rascals. Always somebody is leaping in my bed, and I think it is the banker that kicks at my head. Now perched on ledge as he slides off edge, please don't dig in your claws, don't call in the fall. The hard-dealing crowd will not come aloud to help. In fact, what do you see? Lilacs are pink. Plum. Blue. New. And the look is lush, with a purple passion. Anyway, that's the way to know reality round the border of insanity? Or is it a nuclear fantasy in a shiver of ecstasy? Christ was a black, yes. Will you give him the help that he lacks? It's not enough to chant peace and fuck till the mind falls apart. If our remedies oft in ourselves do lie, there's always a case to be made for running away from your life, for the pleasure of pulling on galoshes, for that cosmic darkness, that yawning chasm. Are you losing your mind? Or is it the singing of your long-lost never had child that brings new beginnings, and helps the world go wild?

I said it already: the way people carry on

you'd think there was something wrong. And most people either don't talk about it at all or, if they do, they put things so vaguely that no one can understand what they mean. Yes, what do they mean? Specifically, every woman is aware that in the vaginal area her body regularly produces moisture. Yet when a sun goddess strolls in the moonlight she wears nothing, because this breeze of flesh-air is pure. And so a little girl's skirt is sexy when a big girl wears it, even though conservative leaders had not realized the steam behind the wage explosion, and how deep-rooted the causes of inflation were or how many big firms were struggling to make ends meet. They took you for the bang-bang-bye-bye type — a quick sweet screw and so long, yes. Instead girls are like honey in a hive. Absolutely. Because the eyes cast round, and the mind seeks harmonized disunities even when the wind is blowing along the slopes and high up, among the gables. In fact the prick of this pick may very well become a new magnet for people seeking the good life. That is to be able to eat something else instead of *vitello tonnato*, though the taxi fare had gone up like ack-ack, and one morning you found yourself peering from the map, a North-West Passage to the Cathay of New Year's airport.

Anyway, the first time I ever set foot in Jersey I was offered, yes, forty dollars from behind. For I was walking rapidly away. Big money for a runaway snatch from college, with only a sexophone packed in her legs. And a crazy Italian took over from there. And my dear let me show you this city tonight. Away from that bed pan of the YWCA, in a powerful motorcycle. Then chez Gaia Scienza; and then a hard-pitched flower into me, in that yellow crazy apartment upstairs. 'Gimmee some, Joe, or I'm gonna kill the first guy I meet,' I would have said if he didn't make me whimper immediately and moan and struggle some before I let him pry my soul apart. I yielded instead, and was spread.

'Oh, Joe, I want to . . . Did you ever hear of Willie? Was he kissed?'

'Shut up!' he hissed, he so hissed, somersaulting all over me, becoming a small ball of naked agony rolling in the sand, clutching, grasping, sucking, blowing, heaving, leaping, and finally, squatting — plop!

'It was the music,' he said. 'Can you hear the band?'

'Yes, I can.'

'Well, that's a disgusting music.'

'I agree,' I replied with conviction. 'It conjures up visions of a piece of meat laid on a platter — or a corpse in a lab. It's so impersonal.'

'It's personal. However, I feel very close to you for some reason. I guess it's just being here on the bed, in the beautiful dawn like this. It's natural, and it's not unreal — it's surreal.'

I nodded, not quite sure what he meant, or that he really meant anything. He was just a young guy being romantic, I guessed. So I let him talk on, and I kept quiet, because he felt like talking on for the time being. And that was freedom. I felt close to him, too, but felt no obligation to say so — and that was freedom, too. When he moved again closer to me for more and more warmth, and noticed that he was still himself, and neither of us commented, that wasn't only freedom. That was totally licence and trust. So I said: 'You know, Joe, I trust you. Want to know why I came to Jersey? It's my first time . . . and still a dove . . . So I thought I'd come here and get finally well-fed in the fen like most of the girls do, and get it over with, you know. But now I realize that Jersey is like a state of mind . . .'

'No, its a trap. You like the bang-bang and the band, uh? Well, I don't like the bang-bang and the band. They have quite a few girls who like the bang-bang and the band. And two of them are from your college, Crystal Baby and Carolyn. Only later, though, they realized that they had ended up with flagpole sitters, but it was too late.'

'Oh, well,' I said. 'They can copy all they can follow. I don't mind. But they can't copy my mind.'

'So you would like to be with them . . .'

'I told you, I don't mind.'

'Imitation is suicide. At any rate, I left 'em sweating and stealing a year and a half behind, though, actually there is no specific cure for migraine.'

'Can you cultivate equanimity, wear glasses if needed? Because I do.'

'I was always a healthy bugger, my dear. However, the best things in resort life are free, and we are talking about a lot more than sun, sand and sea, do you follow me?'

'I see what you mean. Some performers are performers, a few are presences. I've never met Crystal Baby, nor Carolyn . . .'

'Oh, you will. Crystal Baby made a pass at a passing role. And that can happen. And when it does, you swivel. Not every night, but often enough to keep your neck muscles in trim.'

'How uneasy it is to get sucked in by mass hysteria!'

'Yes. How easy it is to become a rhinoceros, to think thick green skin and horns beautiful. But . . . beware of the broad sweep of emotional and transient idolatry. If you become part of the blah-blah-blahs . . .'

'Me? Perhaps you are . . .'

'Never. I'll tell you. The dogs were held back only by ropes tied to the frame of a cannibalized wreck — to rattle their teeth on the windows, to think about why they had developed a sad attitude towards sadness, and a tragic attitude towards tragedy.'

'Whose dogs?'

'Zip's . . . whose life has been full of terrible misfortunes, most of which never happened. You'll see him soon, if you wish.'

'And who's he?'

'The Maestro. He does a stand-up night club routine with amazing precision as well as making love convincingly to a beautifully proportioned guy stripteaser . . . He was ahead of his time in the use of four-letter words. He saw that language would be free when you could say any obscenity without audiences being shocked or a vice squad ready to hand out a warrant. The only bad thing about him is that he worries a lot. And worry is the constant drip, drip, drip of water . . . Do you follow me?'

'Sure, you will die if you keep on crying. Just live each day until bedtime.'

'Oh, life . . . a daylight compartment!'

'Come, gentleman, we sit too long on trifles. What's your name, Joe?'

'*Chiamami Adone.* Or just Joe. Joe Adonis . . . Well, can you invent for me a few quick stories about your life before meeting my motorcycle? Because one has to invent if he wants to keep his place in the band . . . You are a Primrose Bourbon, and I know that you are able to flip your panties with little else to confuse a costume designer. However, imagination is . . .'

'Okay, Joe. A glorious, brief but glorious,

pre-puberty Kierkegaarden age. Best moments spent with one other equally small but eager, tireless body, with a big, a very big . . . a big generous grin. Mutual counselling in times of urinary stress after good hours in a musty old garage, exploring unknown cavities, indents, cracks, crevices . . . whence unanswered queries, and let me look again. Any discoveries of classification were divulged excitedly over bicycle handlebars, in whispers first, growing louder into glee, followed by a vigorous race around schoolyard tamarack, back again for confirmation. There was something vitally delightful in all of that, Joe.'

'Erotic twingers?'

'Definitely. To get back to that musty dark cinder-strewn dusty windowed garage, where already small but confident world becomes more intense, private and intimate.'

'Somebody could peep . . .'

' . . . but no, they wouldn't, slight over-the-shoulder paranoia, then to be summoned from the house just yonder, the concentrated spell broke, overalls up, belts tied, thinking the secret hours . . .'

'There was envy, I suppose, which doesn't exclude delight.'

'Piss in a pop bottle.'

'A brother, a father, a father who smiled when you looked?'

'Moaning spring cats, Joe, moaning alarming agony. Then . . . when hormones still in

143

badminton rackets and giggles and running. A warm summer evening beckoned into a tent. Only dark confusion. Refusal . . .'

'Oh, why?'

'Baseball, road hockey, dry desert of people. Until air injection . . . for there appeared a guy, marvelous, virile, laughing, full of wisdom, eyes that sparkled and gave and enjoyed . . .'

'Joe Adonis, the freak . . . I suppose . . .'

'Officially a school principal. And I watched for four busy years, and blushed, and thoughts blossomed. Adrenaline flowed. He finally focused as a guy! But the thought stayed inside, only music flowed in and out. Coltrane, Parker, Evans, Dolphy, they said it, and got my love, along with many long hours at a violin, eking out the sounds I was hearing. Until a rainy day, the couch soft enveloping, inviting, and nobody came yes nobody came . . . Spring rain, and what are fifty years when . . .?'

'Fifty years? He was fifty years?'

'Hot is the color of two sides by side?'

'Benedetta . . . the smaller the town the faster the nastier the gossip.'

'Yes. They used to call me Lisa. Lisa Jones. And I was yawning. Projection, desire . . . then something else sprouts with flowers, that is wild and for a while insatiable . . .'

'Through any blizzard for more.'

'Oh yes. No hair on the top of his head.

All on that hard strong chest that topped a middle-aged belly, lovable nonetheless . . .'

'Fifty years . . .!'

'Yes. Energies went a lot of places, playing, walking, thinking sixteen-year-old seriousness, fatalism. But for a very long time that man held the center, unfalteringly . . .'

'Unfalteringly.'

'Dreamt little of him except for mild nightmares, where I was Lady Macbeth. Unfortunate that the breasts too negligible for clutching.'

'But the eagle must spread his wings . . . So, now, you're running away . . .'

'Alas the fool . . . And fear of the small town, chase for the big town . . . Very hard to look at young men after that. For they didn't, wouldn't, as I wished . . .'

'Well . . .' he then said, and smiled. We were about to make a deal. And suddenly I discovered something very important. Deep green grass, green smoke, green water, cruising helplessly downwind.

'*Tu sei tu e io sono io,*' he said.

And I: 'What's mine is yours, and what is yours is mine.'

And he: 'What's mine is mine, and what is yours is yours.'

And I: 'Speak what we feel, not what we ought to say.'

And he: 'Hereafter, in a better world than this, I shall desire more love and knowledge of you.'

Yet calm is something filling. Circle complete. Love, and I'll see you in the street. Joe Adonis, yes, is a freak. I'm told not to kill, he said to me that first night, and they kill me. Not to steal, and they steal me from the sun outside. They may be yea of my year, but they're nary nay of my day. Oh, yeah. While I merely want to exist off the carcass of a dying civilization. Right on!

And to him I said: 'Will you make enough for you to reap it? As the day stands up on end how high will you leap?'

And he said: 'Water still runs deep, dark as a dungeon. But life is a sentence that you mumble till the end. And the landlord is an agent that looks like a friend.'

And I said: 'It devils me. Where's the band?'

'Here's a photograph. Watch . . . In threatening colors, whose sun sets . . . on what? An avenue of obelisks and crumbling columns reaches off — to where? Brushed lurid clouds reflect — whatever minds reflect. Why are the crisp clean obelisks arrayed against those ancient columns stretching to a dying day? Who are those figures on the sand, some crouched (afraid?), some upright (enrapt?), and who is that whose back is turned against the patterned world? What sex is hidden in those robes, what age are those tight-folded arms? Why is the column felled and robbed of symbol sun? Perspective leads the eye away, but interest draws it back to one who sits (fragmented?) in the view, who rests, withdraws, or hides beneath external covering of the soul, a dying sun that drops away before the hour of darkness. What one are you, and who are you in this stark canvas?'

I was fascinated, and didn't answer.

Also now energies went lot of places, playing, walking. And for a long long time Joe Adonis held one center only. Unfalteringly. Unfortunate that the breast too negligible for clutching. Innocent as the babe unborn.

And so — because I wanted to — he introduced me to the band.

'Oh, well,' he said, 'a bare back is the best bit to present to the mob . . .'

And nobody could save him. Neither I. And now, when I look below, pressing my nose to the window pane, hiding my pain, I still try to catch a glimpse of him as he runs to the border in a cloud of gunfire . . . But he is gone. So then, if you are going to tie the tie that binds, you might as well follow the crowd to the woods. They pile into smoke and find the fire. But I love you Joe. This is why I'm going to spill every lust bean in the can.

XXI

Yes, Crystal. Must pull off clothes to jerk like a frog, on belly and nose, from the sucking bog? My meat eats me. Who waits at the gate? I kiss her moving mouth, her swart hilarious skin. She breaks my breath in half. She frolics like a beast. What's freedom for? Let seed be grass, and grass turn into hit. I'm martyr to a motion not my own. Money money money. Water water water. Like a slither of eels that watery chick kisses my tongue, and my lips awake. But wait! Where the weeds slept? I'm too abstract, Joe? I must be more correct. Was it dust I was kissing? Alone, perhaps, I was kissing the skin of a stone. I shall start then, from the beginning. This business of the band. This Zip the Thunder's Band. In all honesty.

First perception. The first judgment was true and right. Second, third and ensuing judgments were stupid by prejudice — the judge being bribed, poked at, eaten, nibbled at, sat upon. Presented with a photograph labelled 'Zip the Thunder's Untouchable Seven Sages Band', I reacted with horror. A truly truly negative reaction, plus a smile — uncontrolled.

But, you know, even if an idea is forced, it

is a defensive idea. So all the more so in its realization. And yet it was realized, which I suppose illustrates a truism of some sort. A conception, I mean, can be. There is no saying that something cannot be conceived just because it's deformed, or defective. Do you follow me? A defensive idea because, yes, all girls can make as much sound as well as a bunch of men. The importance of the sound. Music recedes before the fact of sex. And at first sight Zip has such a winning smile! Zip, caught in the living death of his own creation. But that first encounter — *what a fantastic lady!* Can say only yes to Her, to Him. Then a job. Playing sexophone. And money. And she said: 'Oh you'll have a ball, child Benedetta.'

And I meet the Band, see them.

(An aside — but that first photograph told me: 1) no way; 2) no hip, no light in the eyes; 3) jive, jive, jive; 4) probably sick — I mean all girls. How fukt-up can you get?)

Cold, giving little, and me hoping that at last I may express some enthusiasm for music and get some response. Musicians, you know! But no, no, no. Brick wall. Thump. Nothing. Jersey life. Is this the fabulous Jersey life?

And the band: 'What kind of music do you play?'

'Mumble mumble.'

But mostly silence. And unwillingness, that is: 'We know where we're at, chick. Don't bother us.'

And there they are, without exception, at the bar. Yes, I am naive. What the hell do they do at the bar all these hours? Yes, they must be drinking. But night after night after night?

I suppose it was fear. I heard of death. Of people getting killed. I lived with deep roots once. Have I forgotten their ways? Yet we rush into a rain that rattles double glass. And beyond the mountain pass mist deepens on the pane. I began to be insane. But I wouldn't say it. I still wanted to stretch the wind with a stick.

On that train to New York I first met Crystal, the girl about whom Zip had said: 'Oh what a beautiful musician: she knows everything Madame Pompadour knew.'

And who was she? The rags of my anatomy?

Crystal was huge and had violent facial features. And her smile gave nothing, offered nothing, as if a volcano not erupting — but come too close, and it would. And I thought yikes! egads! But *this* woman — lover jazz they told me. *If* she does. How in my terms does she love music and life and outrage? So I left an opening that fought all that my eyes and good sense told me, despite the fact that one cannot expect wonders with new people. How to improve?

We were doing one hour show then, for rich elderly people, mouth upon mouth, singing — my lips pressed upon stone. Which meant day after day empty, unless a library searched out, a book to read, a letter to write.

Then interminable waiting at the club we play till show time, watching lousy cabaret acts, an old house of cats, with saxifrage and fern at the edge of a raw field.

The first sensations sitting in their midst, on stage, were probably due to prolonged absence from such contexts. A few years and more since I had sat with a band that size of that ilk — brass, sex. The lights frightened me. The sound took me aback. And it was all over before I had time to take it in.

But newness gone, one becomes accustomed. The blasé grows. And so life is, people wise, next to nil. Only Carolyn, the *pianissimo* pianist compared with Rube Bloom, has an ear, a listening simpatico ear. But even she warms slowly to my babble about music — my enthusiasm! Do we not often grant a person so much more just out of generosity on our part? Hello, hello! My nerves knew you, dear boy. Have you come to unhinge my shadow? Last night, you know, I slept in the pits of a tongue. Wrong, oh wrong! Our generosity compensating — really actually — for a real, actual lack in that person? Once granted, we take that as our perception of him. And so musically is dead too.

But a light — Crystal Baby, lead alto, who alone plays consistently with balls, nerves, beauty sometimes. It is the ravage that Jersey had already wreaked upon me after Joe's escape to Italy that made me, allowed me to value that senselessly, with uncontrolled admiration, envy too? A sole release, so paltry really; but I felt there was hope in that. Let the kisses resound, flat like a butcher's palm.

The first conversation with that chic, on the train to New York, impressed me. She impressed me as being exceedingly bitter. Found it hard to talk, perhaps because she didn't listen. I suppose then was the first shit I took as well. No! But the foundations laid.

Question: why oh why, if at the onset I was able to perceive all that chic? Shit for chic, chic for shit? I mean it was all chic from the start. It stank. There was nothing, only the allure of regular money. And I didn't fuck it then. Why persist and say: 'Well, I'll back it awhile, hack it awhile?' And I mothered in the chic, asked for more, and yes started producing it. Death too comes silently, surreptitiously, with complacency, curiosity. Light takes the Tree; but who can tell us how? The lowly worm climbs up a winding staircase; I wake to sleep, and take my waking slow. Did I learn by going where I have to go?

And yes, I began to drink more often, more copiously. The one avenue it seemed, to the heads, hearts, livers, to the rest. So one simply joins in on the haze. More deception. Tongues loosen. But in the after haze of the mornings following, it is as if naught had taken place. All can be cancelled, if drunkenness was the medium.

'But we were so drunk!'

Two themes dominate for a while. One is drinking — a new experience partially through the group nature of it, partially through the excessive nature of it. The second: that *one* musical light, Crystal Baby.

There develops an interpersonal necessity, felt towards her. Almost always from a cold distance which she put there, I watched the impetuosity, which I took for fire; the hilarity drunken, which I took for spirit, unabashed spirit of outrage. And in that musical void that is the Organization of Zip the Thunder she played something, so it was beauty, solid, creative.

And what anxious process began to grow in this admiration? This woman, producing sounds equal to those I'd lived so long with, and at the same time promising more — and this in such glaring contrast to the surrounding! I suppose the pain and wrongness of it struck deep. Somehow the beauty — fineness of the music — became all the more so for that, and exaggerated even to the point of transferring the painfulness to the source, this woman. Feeling her deeply through myself. So grows a desire, a wish to touch, to lift. The desire is so strong as to be blind. In darkness, wants to see light. So bows down blindly, stupidly and says: 'Steamroller, roll, if you will.' She turns, as if to go, half-bird, half-animal. The wind dies on the hill.

The beginnings were in essence a portent of the outcome. They had the making of the wrong outcome. But in themselves the beginnings were fresh, as spring lilacs, and they promised goodness. True light shone from those usually dark, clouded eyes. Why a desire to touch where nobody should desire to touch? I lived with open sound, aloft, and on the ground.

Intention is to give, offer a hand, as one would do on the way up a steep embankment. Not to cut off the hand, for it's useless that way. Perhaps the uselessness dead end came first, then expressed its desperation in the womb, that lovely flower. Desperation for life. Wanted to give that release, that could be a freeing release, release each other from our clutches.

No. A willing victim, blind to the fact that she understood little about herself. So, therefore, little about others.

About her: from what I may glean, crucial factor is thus this, that in those most impressionable and important years fifteen, sixteen, eighteen, through luck perhaps, I was treated to a solid, formative foundation of judgment values meeting all manner of fine people (background). And it seems in all that time — while I was given so much, experienced so much, learned so much — she met: 1) musicians who are not necessarily hip or anything of the like; 2) one man who probably remains *the one ex-*

perience. All led to that. Now all leads to that. The vortex circling indeed. Vacuum Vortex. Yes, in the earlier stages I must admit to a new fascination with womb. There being so much of it all together at once, and it had been for years, as well! A second thought that, a perverted one essentially, I mean count those hours that they all spend together on that stand! Can the rays of sun on skin be denied?

I ask you.

XXII

The ego. That which demands, is its own advertisement, and indicates or signifies nothing but itself. In a situation where there is neither interest nor intelligence nor life, there is one huge bellowing ego. Its volume, mistaken for definitiveness; space occupied by matter, mistaken for substance. And the ant carries a brick wall on its back.

Must I return to the *defensive* idea again? Is the importance of music secondary to that of the sex of the musician? Then this is an idea that must be offered, proffered in such a way as to assume the openness to music, and to push the all-female aspect forward either as a frivolous entertainment, boobs on a post card, or on the serious side, as female musicians, which is nothing in itself, only something in the fact that they are together in a band. That is the defensiveness of women's lib.

The brick wall. The washerwoman. It becomes clear that through her bigness of ego — selfishness on the one hand — it expressed the only pathos, injustice. I mean she lives it on the stage. The others sit quietly in the muck, the only variation being from sober to somewhat drunk, to pissed. *All* are wrapped around poison Zip's finger. Only Crystal bellows about it, knows it, does not like it, but has lived with it so long, thrives on it, knows nothing else. Being wrapped around poison Zip's finger means you can laugh, giggle, tomfool about, 'have a good time', and curse Zip and complain and grumble and have a row with Zip — even get sacked threatened. The pettiness of it all is essential to its inward deadly continuation. Pettiness breeds pettiness and hypocrisy breeds hypocrisy but keeps the walls standing. Does anyone shout out injustice, foul stinking stench? No. No one, except perhaps to herself, and slowly she forgets, talking to herself being so unfruitful.

Deception. Defensive and deceptive as with the bottle. Alcohol. Drugs. It symbolizes (popularly) glamour, sex, good times, party time, party glow. Its reality is a mumbling razy tongue, a lizard's eyes, glibness, easiness in words, flattery, moving wandering easy hands. Knowing not what to do, wait (in close to willessness) for something to happen, in limp nowhere for a spark. Double chins and protruding bellies, these tell, and gray bagged eyes. The blanched vacant morning face over a boiled egg. This tells, this is the reality of the bottle. Sure the laughter comes more easily and abundantly and there is an approximation, a sense of, *maybe* even a striving for camaraderie, oneness through the haze, by the haze, stumblers occur and provoke laughter. And all of this provides meat for the constant conversation of reminiscence. There's room for a rest though, a rest for aching heads, cloudy, low-functioning heads. Yes, there may be a lull — this just long enough to nurture the recurring desire to fill the (restful) void, again once more, with the easiest filler.

Mistake. Essential mistake is to assume that because I am there, in that void, it is no longer a void, an emptiness, a rottenness — or it is less so. From there, the vain attempt to prove this to myself: 'Sure it sucks, but it's not that bad.'

No. One can't deny the rays of the sun on the skin.

No. One can't deny hours spent with nine or ten other wombs. The womb focuses bigger.

One drunk evening at the Club, friendly, a few rounds. But Crystal and Annette kept to themselves, seemingly engrossed in deep conversation. They left before the rest.

On returning home, the signs, the car, and light in my (our) room. Tiddly, not walking straight, giggly, intoxicated, I am — and even titillated to think I might giggle with Annette and Crystal who are probably in the front room, a kitchen. The door to my own room, shut. But I barge in to doff my bag and coat. My eyes perceive one white long tall body — backside, blond-haired, on top of Crystal's big brown body. Flash, flash, flash in my head. Wait a minute. Regret first, a sort of embarrassment, but *no* disapproval, *no* reproach.

Annette left, apologizing. Crystal threw her head on my shoulder. 'Save me, save my soul!' She cried, she shook, she tried to talk. I was cool and reasonable. Babbled about sensuality of course, missing the point. What the hell with those two in particular, how did they get there?

And Crystal still more drunk than I, after the 'discussion' exchange let's say, she stripped and invited me to sketch. She posed. I looked greedily at a very smooth skin, the outline of the body so smooth, sleek, fine. The limbs finely shaped, even the excess finding a place. She offered this to my eyes and a hand with pencil delighted in it. I took it no further, consciously. Still separate and unencroaching.

The boisterous actress, buffoon in her returned. Did she bring what ate at her, was eating at her? Which she wanted burned out, 'out damned spot.' Bury it in hilarity. The mirror of the other girls just waiting, to laugh. Conditioned response under the influence of alcohol.

Violence, in its beginnings. The awkward movements made deliberately — and deliberately ask for attention and response. They sometimes are deliberate and violent and want only attention, a particular attention, *deference* to a vile demanding yet impossible to alleviate, temper. Crystal the Boss. Only way to live with it. That too is part of the much.

I'm being very harsh with this woman. She did show some love. But was it just a clever concession to get more attention? Pessimism is so much easier than optimism. There's no work to being a pessimist.

Those periods of sobriety — she would read, and drink tomato juice. The solos were not just bombastic, but clear, proportioned, fine and even moving to my open ears, starving ears. And hands, ears that wanted to do the same and better. There is outrage in quality alone, in such a context. In other words, quality amidst shit spells outrage. (How dare you?) And amidst that same shit, it often goes unnoticed. So we add to the tragedy of it all.

Zip the Thunder, the enveloping cushion, the insistent vacuum cleaner, the hammer that falls and falls and falls. And she cares primarily for her own convenience. Only a greater guy, or should I say only a great transvestite could lift the level higher than that. It's been reduced to a matter of convenient survival. He said, 'The line up doesn't matter, love. I could just as well do without a sexophone, have a rhythm guitar.' He's indifferent to form. Absolutely indifferent as far as form itself is concerned. It matters only if it will still sell, and still sound. Stop. I am related to Eddie Lang — Joe Venuti, and Bix with Tram and Eddie.

XXIII

She lives upstairs in a cast. Eyes spread out like spinning eggs. That rug smells already of moth dust. Ooh, Cinderella. The ugliest girl in town. But listen to this. The Mice ate up our ambassador and six diplomatic aides, Sir. Shall we lower the flag to half-mast?

BOOT: 'What the hell happened? How did Sissy walk in there like that? Did you tell him to walk in to Dog?'

BRUNO: 'We set it up, Boot.'

BOOT: 'Why did he, Sissy, make a statement that he did this more or less?'

BRUNO: 'Because that girl, Edna, took the whole rap.'

BOOT: 'Well, yeah, according to the County Medical Examiner Signor Strano, she's the one that did . . .'

BRUNO: 'She didn't hit him in the head.'

BOOT: 'But he, Sissy, he's going to be an accessory. He'll wind up with a bit.'

BRUNO: 'Sure.'

BOOT: 'Who squealed on him? How did they know he was there?'

BRUNO: 'They had him, Sissy, nailed, fingerprints and all. Then Bobby "Big-Flag-Pole" Elzeviro went around screaming about it.'

BOOT: 'That rat!'

BRUNO: 'What did Lou and them have to butt in there for? I just don't know.'

BOOT: 'Did they come to the old guy when they told him?'

BRUNO: 'No. Pimple Boy grabbed hold of Sissy down there.'

BOOT: 'Oh, down there.'

BRUNO: 'He talked to Sissy and Sissy sent word to Magoo, in Philadelphia.'

BOOT: 'It's about time Sissy told Magoo to have his guys mind their own business.'

BRUNO: 'So Pimple Boy came back on Monday and went down again.'

BOOT: 'Well, if we get a good judge, he'll get a small bit. What was he doing up in that joint, and who was this broad? That girl, Edna, had a junkie rap and everything.'

BRUNO: 'He met this broad and she used to go out with this — '

BOOT: 'Who?'

BRUNO: 'The guy that got killed.'

BOOT: 'Oh, she must have wanted him to go in that joint.'

BRUNO: 'Yeah, she did. But she stood up just as good as he did.'

BOOT: 'I hear it is the truth.'

BRUNO: 'It is. Thus that guy started making up to her and she pushed him.'

BOOT: 'Big-Flag-Pole must be dying. The

first time he opens a gambling joint. He's a dirty tail wagging — He's been that way all his life, he had a lot of people killed — '

To hear this. I didn't scream. But I knew. And I said: 'You got to go out of my life, okay?' Where they came from? However, a blood and barricades revolution will not work in this day and age, because they have more blood and more barricades than we.

But life's not paying when heading for the hills. When you speed up pills believing to learn how to forget you are wet.

And to Joe I once said, raging: 'Your god is chained on a steeple, because you didn't cut down your hang-ups. You study the animals. See how they run. So you make love to people just for fun? This is a beautiful land, Joe. And they're spoiling it.'

And to me he said: 'Yes. The Big Three in Detroit spent $1.5-billion to change their 1970 models. In other words, the Big Three spent more than a billion and a half dollars to make their 1970 models seem new and different in appearance. The effect of this massive annual snow job has been to lock out competitors, understand?'

I understand. But life's road is narrow and full of trials. Abuse of rudimentary cleanliness is blind reaction to an antiseptic society. But Joe, this dark day I lie awake, unable to sleep. And I'm dreaming of you, imagining you underneath me, inside me, over me. And though

I honestly thank you for your wish to me of freedom, I accept that wish and I take it and I wish it for others. I take also all your kisses and return them. I suppose I'm more than a little happy with that morsel. Pain felt in my chest. And I say excellent, excellent. I almost want to be sick going roaring around myself. What the heck with this bird nest? I shall set fire to it.

SILLY: 'Small Fly and I will take Lou back to his car, okay?'

ZIP: 'Fine.'

SILLY: 'Then I'll come over there.'

ZIP: 'Where?'

SILLY: 'To the Club.'

ZIP: 'Well, you have to take him home.'

SILLY: 'Lou? Either home or wherever he leaves his . . .'

ZIP: 'All right, bring him there. Are you gonna put it in the garage?'

SILLY: 'Oh, yeah. I'll get it in.'

ZIP: 'Have you got enough room to work in?'

SILLY: 'If everything is ready, I don't even have to bring it all the way in.'

ZIP: 'You haven't got it all the way in?'

SILLY: 'I won't pull it in now, Zip. After, I'll pull it in.'

ZIP: 'You should have it in there.'

SILLY: 'Doesn't it look funny if a car is in there?'

ZIP: 'Why?'

SILLY: 'This guy, hasn't he got any suspicion about anything?'

ZIP: 'No. Have the hood up. Like you're putting oil or something in there. Understand? This way you know it fits in there and all.'

SILLY: 'Oh, it fits in. Don't worry about it.'

ZIP: 'Have you tried it?'

SILLY: 'I haven't tried the car but I've had the trucks in there.'

ZIP: 'Did your boys get back?'

SILLY: 'Not yet . . . don't worry about it. If they come back, I'll work it out. Small Fly and I figured it out already.'

ZIP: 'How?'

SILLY: 'I'll take him in the office and I'll just tell the boys. How long will it take you to get to the Club?'

ZIP: 'I'll go down there after . . .'

SILLY: 'Okay. Well, we'll drop Lou off. By the time I change the plates and everything . . .'

ZIP: 'Got the pliers and everything?'

SILLY: 'You're gonna have Lou to get rid of them. I'll keep the money and whatever else he brings. And I'll give Lou the clothes . . . shoes . . .'

ZIP: 'Silly, for god's sake, don't get took. This is all gonna . . . you can expect me — I'm gonna wait for the phone call.'

SILLY: 'Okay. We'll put the car outside, all right? We'll leave the key in the ignition and he just has to take it away.'

ZIP: 'Tell Small Fly not to be a cowboy . . . make sure . . .'

SILLY: 'Don't want to use rope? You don't want to use a rope? He said he kisses better with his arm. He can handle it better with his arm.'

ZIP: 'Well, you have a rope already anyhow. But make sure, Silly. Make sure they don't touch nothing out of—'

SILLY: 'Zip, don't hold me responsible. But Zip, let me make . . . this guy's supposed to have a lot of money on him. I hope he's got it on him . . .'

ZIP: 'You got a New York licence? Are your pistols registered over there? Fine, fine. Make sure everything is done when it is done. Pull that car right in now.'

SILLY: 'I would be true, Zip, for there are those who trust me. I would be pure, for there are those who care. I would be strong, for there is much to suffer. I would be brave, for there is much to dare.'

ZIP: 'Get lost!'

The good father with the twinkling in his eye always has cakes in his pocket to bethroat us with for our allmichael good. And I observe that he makes wry faces.

Why, anyway, think about it? The Small Fly never had a chance. He seems to have been invented for the sole purpose of becoming extinct, and that is all he is good for. Homogenuine. Homogeneity. But he used to ask questions, always. What does the word *planet* mean? A wonderer, silly, I would say. Which insects are organized into social groups in which there is a division of labor? Housefly, silly, I would say. Why do male pee-cock spread their feathers? To supply oxygen, silly, I would say. Then Joe said, 'A few moments of silence for people who are still smoking.' So now I'm fully persuaded that nothing is infamous but virtue and public spirit. Because people afraid of dying carry guns, and guns are what people get killed with. Oh America, America! Strange power is no power. But they say, 'There is a little more and there is a little less. Try to get hold of an enemy before you strike a match.' Joe said, however, 'It's hard to fight when you're laughing.' True. Pure in love and in fight died before daylight. And now the soul's crying from a misty grave, living in this tomb of living deads. Sometimes I see only through the madness of mad mad guys who kiss and trap measuring words love and god.

Hot is the odor of two side by side?

Adonai, morrai!

Joe told me of Zip. 'For three months I hunted him. I wanted to kill him, oh yes. The happiest time of my childhood. And then I couldn't. I was too frightened. If I had killed him my life would have been totally different. No children, no family, no work. On the other hand try Asia for assphalt body with the concreke sould and the forequarters of the moon behinding out of his phase.'

And they kicked him, instead. In the head.

XXIV

The wind brings clouds, and rain makes Jersey new. Crystal Baby came in and said: 'Read *The Pearl*, honey. A Journal of Voluptuous Reading.'

And to her I said: 'You have underground up every morning, Crystal, stretching your body with pride, and now you feel nothing is left but nakedness you won't hide.'

She sighed: 'Benedetta, dear. How lovely the honeysuckle smells! You shan't have the nightdress yet.'

And I, knowing the end-game: 'Well, you shall catch it if you want to play.'

'O.K., little chit. I always mean what I say. Your bottom shall smart for it. There, there! Carolyn, did you ever see anyone so hairy as I am?'

'For sure. It's a sign of a loving nature.'

'You see, Carolyn, I love to caress the little featherless birdies like this kid Benedetta.'

And Carolyn: 'She must sleep with me sometimes.'

'Nay, nay!'

'Oh yes,' Crystal Baby said. 'You shall be "slappee" with your birch, Benedetta. I know how to use it properly, especially on naughty bottoms, which have the impudence to challenge me.'

'Ohi, ohi!'

'Do you feel that . . . and that . . .? Is that too hard, or perhaps you like that better? Your bottom must be cut to pieces, if I can't subdue such a proud spirit. There-there-there . . .!'

'How cruelly you have warmed my poor bottom. I'm not in love with you, what's for?'

'Never mind, Benedetta. You got to change your evil ways, babe. Have you really seen worse than that, Carolyn?'

'Oh far, far worse. I've seen the blood flow freely from cut-up bottoms . . .'

'There, there,' Crystal went on. And to Carolyn: 'Now you will nip me, uh? Yes, squeeze that little bit of flesh . . . Please rub, rub . . .'

Finally I said: 'Out, out of my life . . . You don't make a getaway in a semi-trailer. My friends will catch you before you reach fourth gear.'

'Your friends? Joe Adonis is in exile, and Holiday Inn is dead. Who are your friends? Wham-O-Frisbee?'

'The Bronx guys . . .'

'That ridiculous cocksman Fosco Fiaschetti? He had a rolling, slightly bow-legged walk. His black boots glistened in the sun. Yes. But he lives in places where broken things are patched with masking tape. And he butts his head against a wall like a rat in a maze. Understand? The guys in the Bronx are what you might call a perishable commodity. Zip knows it better.'

My face was lumpy. But they went out. The rehearsal was just fine. But not long enough as they wanted it to be. Dirty girls, thumb stump. With a certain sycophantic earnestness and candor. Two priggish reactionaries. But I don't have the courage to be dirty on my own merits, even if the delicious taste and very much indeed satisfying flavor of wringles spermgum gives enjoyment to millions daily. Hoo boy! No one knows all the answers. But I still have my Joe, and what he left here. A purple face with black whiskers sticking out all over. Just don't pull the knot tight before being certain that you have got hold of the right end. But . . . do things that are represented have to exist in order to be represented? I'm in pain, which is not the only pebble on this beach.

It is obvious, then, that the Nine of Cups is always called the wish card. You can't leave a guy hanging in mid-air, Zip the Thunder used to say. And I say, a woman may have true beliefs and yet be irrational. What are, then, the true connections between tolerance, rationality, and liberation? Out of these materials we have produced a theory that invokes the great names of freedom and reason while betraying their substance at every important point. Thus I would say that by performance I mean, in part, any self-discovering, self-watching, finally self-pleasing response to the pressure and difficulties I've been mumbling about. But on the corporate level you clog our Courts with your reluctance to pay taxes. You subvert the interests of our politicians with contributions we cannot hope to match. The harvest you reap goes elsewhere. And when the harvest ends you go with it. Bye, bye, Joe Adonis. After the refusal of all anesthetics what is left to us, please, in order to rebel?

Abbiamo solo questo sporco linguaggio con cui non capire.

In fact, there are no commercials on television selling sanitary products. Too dirty for FCC. It is a kind of guy xenofobia. And if you get sick and tired of nicks on your shin-bones and ankles you have electrolysis done to remove the hair. So, there, lie flat on your back, your legs extended straight ahead, your feet approximately two feet apart, your toes pointed.

Again defensive. And this Club with the band, on top of the hill, a stone-walled garden, hawthorn adorning it. A view (strained) of New York. Everyone knows the gestures that contribute to making the semblance of a coherent existence. So the kitchen larder was well-stocked. The evening meals prepared, eaten with relish enthusiasm, but mostly my enthusiasm. Their enthusiasm minimal and though I had pushed it deep into the nether parts of my memory — it rang false anyway.

Condom. Have a condom, please!

The point is that this isn't self-righteous. The point of the whole story, dammit. Mealtime activity dwindled to the perfunctory. And then sustained in nervousness. The nervous, the restless, perhaps this kind of energy is the last, the bottom of the bucket, in lives that are otherwise bored, empty. It's a sign of good health and cerebral movement included at least of course, but this does not imply either thought, or consideration, or creation (a thought is a creation). And is not a healthy (well-fed) body a defense? And people visited and came and went. And sat in sober silence. Thank god for coffee and cigarettes and TV. And how often in the absence of these visitors, I would see sleep for no other reason than something to do. And how often heard it said, 'I am bored.' The bored are also boring! Are these not signs of death?

Zip provides purpose, places to go, to be at, he provides life for us all. We accept begrudgingly on the surface, more thankful deeper down. So the verbal shitting on one another between Zip and the band, which is a symbiotic relationship, once in awhile somebody busts the line, does the unusual, and this move, which rocks the boat, grinds, churns out more chic in its wake, necessarily thanks to Zip. He cannot let you depart, exit just smeared, but must throw more at you.

A quote (from a recent letter from my

mother): 'We stayed overnight at Picton, and thought it rather rundown, so were surprised to see it had a girl's band.'

Another: 'Yeah write it all down, you're going to need it someday.'

Venom, spite. What for?

And now . . . they are downstairs. And he must be Pimple Boy. Oh mind the door, mind the door!

XXV

PIMPLE BOY: 'So what's new?'

ZIP: 'Oh, a little trouble over there, in the Bronx.'

PIMPLE BOY: 'In the Bronx?'

ZIP: 'Yeah. Close the door. Nobody's supposed to know.'

PIMPLE BOY: 'Zip, if you don't want to tell me you don't have to tell me.'

ZIP: 'It's about Fosco Fiaschetti and his *brigata*. The Commission don't like the way he's comporting himself after the dethroning of Joe Adonis.'

PIMPLE BOY: 'The way he's conducting himself, you mean?'

ZIP: 'Well, he wants to come here and destroy the band. I feel sorry for the guy, you know. He's not a bad guy. But he wants to kiss me and the Organization.'

PIMPLE BOY: 'He's got no intentions, as far as I know.'

ZIP: 'Oh yeah? He arranged for a casket, put it aboard the *Michelangelo*, and then made arrangements with the steamship company — in the event of my death — to put my corpse in a freezing compartment and keep it there till the liner returns home.'

PIMPLE BOY: 'You mean . . . he wants to return you to Italy in a casket?'

ZIP: 'Those guys in the Bronx, ah! They find their minds so solaced with their own flights that they neglect the study of growing rich. Besides, they are for the most part mighty lovers of their palates, and this is known an impoverisher. Their grossest fault is that you may conclude them sensual. Yet this does not touch them at all.'

PIMPLE BOY: 'These guys all confused . . .'

ZIP: 'I want to tell you something, Pimple Boy. You're a soldier . . .'

PIMPLE BOY: 'That's all I am. But I don't wanna be a soldier mamma, I don't wanna die.'

ZIP: 'You see, these people . . . I mean, the people in Fosco's *brigata* — none of them wants to open his mouth about him . . . I feel sorry for the situation.'

PIMPLE BOY: 'What do you mean, there isn't one guy in our group?'

ZIP: 'In our Administration . . . Well, I sat down with four or five of them and the best I got was hello and good-buy. The rest of them are at attention.'

PIMPLE BOY: 'It could be that they're a hundred percent loyal to their boss and they want to stay with him.'

ZIP: 'Pimple Boy, there's nobody that wants

peace and harmony more than me. You know that. I feel life, I feel love.'

PIMPLE BOY: 'I'm with you! But how can I go forward when I don't know which way I'm facing?'

ZIP: 'Pimple Boy, I'm telling you because tomorrow I don't want to see you get involved in anything. I want you to know that the Commission has nothing against any of your people.'

PIMPLE BOY: 'Zip, maybe I don't understand . . .'

ZIP: ' . . . cause this is strictly off the record. It's between you and me, but tomorrow I don't want you to say, "Jesus Christ, I hold mama as a friend and she don't let me know!" Imagine all the people living for today . . .'

PIMPLE BOY: 'I understand that, Zip. But you're only as good as the team you're on. You're with the team — win, lose or draw! How can I go forward when I don't know which way to turn? How can I go forward into something I'm not sure of?'

ZIP: 'Wait a minute, Pimple Boy. I'm not asking—'

PIMPLE BOY: 'I know that! You say to me that "in the event something happens I don't want to see you involved." How do I duck? What kind of a jerk would I be to duck? You know life can be long, and you got to be strong, and the world is so tough sometimes I feel I've had enough.'

ZIP: 'Well, you see, Pimple Boy, as long as nobody gets hurt . . .'

PIMPLE BOY: 'See what I mean? Maybe I don't understand you!'

But I do understand you, Zip! You have disgraced Sicily and Italy in America. You fear to die. And to you I say, Joe is coming, Joe is coming . . . Never hate mere pork which is bad for your knife of a good Friday. Never slip the silver key through your gate of golden age. Collide with guy, collude with money. So I went there once, in the Bronx, in disguise. Looking for him. They told me Joe had come back. But I didn't see him. And thought I was in an airline terminal. It was like seeing a movie in a refrigerator. That menstrual bleeding somehow weakens a woman. And there I see old Italians who had studied with Jung, and violinists from the Balkans. Fosco said to wait and wait. So I would sit in the airy, still light of a Caravaggio's studio, wondering at it all sadly, reading on the red walls, swallowing my pain.

But, of course, the problem after a war is with the victor. Zip the Thunder thinks he has just proved that war and violence pay. And so who will now teach him a lesson? Joe is coming, Joe is coming . . . A desperate population is dominated by the Lavanda, strong through its political connections, but we begin to seek possible remedies, because you have to suffer to be beautiful. Finally I know that. Only Joe can prevail in the common struggle. Because when abstraction sets to killing you, you've got to get busy with it. Ham and Oedipus?

I felt impersonal, as if I were making love in the abstract. Thus she became queen, and, as the king said when he presented her to the nobles at the Court, she surpassed in virtue and loveliness all the women in his realm. We eat of a halcyon paste. It is green as the artichoke heart. And she still keeps her eyes on tomorrow, because it helps you shake your future.

Now slowly, imperceptibly, the days began to shorten, the grass turned brown. I traced their lines with my fingers, following along the hollows they made, raising the soft hair like fur, and then smoothing it down again as it became longer and began to buck in the grasp. I'm still dreaming of you.

Shem is death. And Shem is that. With all the wisdom and all the pain. But, of course, you can take home even murder, and play it over and over again.

In which our little life is grown for sleep.

XXVI

Then suddenly he walked into this mush of unawareness, Joe Adonis, with his physicians of the Bronx: the *Normale Società* to take care of the *Gaia Società*. And he immediately knew with clarity that it was all a pile of atrocious obscenity.

A guy in every sense, full, complete, strong, with roots and wings, a sense of humor, always there, clarity of vision, of perception, perspicacity — always there. He entered over this world of stagnant pools of trapped women and guysters pretending to be otherwise like moonlight and starlight to frighten owls and mortal eyes. And a purge came.

Stage one of the recovery. Crystal Baby hurried up, and threatened, said, 'You have a finger on my soul. Do something.' She shot in my face all the while. And did I take it, and then more, and said:

'Come with me, with us.' And more garbage did she eject at our feet.

Joe talked to her with grace, sullen ungiving, close-eared she was. Then tears, which was regeneration, having had enough a small relief.

That guy so fine! He let her touch him,

abuse him, use him roughly. And me sick, sick with the knowledge inside that it should have been thus. But there, there was no desperation. It was simply and uncomplicatedly moral sexual exchange, no more no less, nobody wanted anything from another. There were no such lumps sticking at the pit of anybody's stomach. No heavy painful weights in anyone's head, no head was shaking no, no, no.

I walked her home in the morning. We parted there. Then, and that was the last tenderness, however false or fucked up it was. The last tender glance, the mouth gun: kiss. Oh, beware of the tender kiss between women, but generally beware of it any time; for it's not poison, it is pregnant overflows with poisonous potential. It portends what is too sweet, sickly. Kills. But she spared me, the redeemer redeemed.

Oh this guy, my Joe! He pulled the foul rug from beneath me, hit me, bit me hard, loved me lovingly. And took no shit. He blew the breath of life back into me. And to her Joe.

Tears: were the first sign. They came hot and plentiful such as they wanted to for so long, and with frequency. I am radiant in the very dead of winter.

It wasn't just lovemaking, pure, simple and predictable, of the many dimensional mind frolic. No, no. So much more and better and complete than that. There was no derobing ritual, no, no. The starting point was purity of intent, togetherness: and from there no modesty allowed and no modesty necessary.

Let's take the shining of the apple. And the forms of polishing ready for eating. Some of that could be harsh, hard and soft with consent. But most of that was sight and smell, hearing and touch and taste, pumping, humping, thumping. We fly. And oh my love for the first time in my life my eyes are wide open. And oh my love for the first time in my life my eyes can see. No romantic flings. Only natural links. A love never wavered. A careful progeny. A being together so clean and strong I thought often while we tossed that frisbee about between us — the laughter, the sweat pouring off us — and the accompanying joy which simply comes closer, bigger when we are physically closer, it is integral to that joy.

Have I not mentioned how not only did this guy grace a toilet seat as any other seat? He allowed me the same freedom. I was a queen on any throne, let's say. So was he king.

And they all loved him; even if they disapproved perfunctorily, all those females and guysters loved him, and would have liked to sidle closer, forgetting their glitter and sharpening the tooth of the dog, the red river of corpses, resurrection so near.

One very young and hipless girl of fifteen used to ogle him across the hotel dining room. All part of the surrounding: outside nonsense, incoherence, silliness that passes for proper so-

185

cial behavior! The ogling progressed to an out-right attack. A little red mouth plants itself on the knowing and generous mouth of this, my Man. Reaction — the only decent thing to do, to at least return the gesture. He reaches to touch this tiny body, and tiny indeed it was! The telling of this provoked giggles.

'How mielodorous is thy bel chant,' Miss Tiny said.

He to her: 'A washable lovable floatable doll, if you loll, and one must sell it to some-one, the sacred name of love, uh?'

'Yes, oh yes. My only desire is to be slipped on, to be slept by, to be conned to, to be kept up.'

Witty, too. While the older ladies kept their distance. But I know they watched with keen interest the frisbee game. And so they watched the guy in the striped multi-colored trousers stroll the street, his rather strange walk, *hered-itatis columna erecta*, order a drink. Who'll buy me penny babies?

The right care will make any plant grow, and become what it could and should. Some of me looks its age but the bosom region has always lacked sadly. But oh did these bosoms begin to smile beneath his hands? The polish-ing was never-ending, only in separation have the smiling bosoms waned. To look out from the privacy of inside, onto blue sky and rich blue sea. And a lush Jersey green coast. This spacious gift to the eye makes the soaring higher.

He said, in his second coming, but chanting: 'I've seen fire and I've seen rain, Benedetta. And I've seen lonely times. But I always thought that I'd see you one more time again.'

In the middle of the night I call his name. And now spring is not enough for us.

XXVII

But look, look: what is hot, liquid rock? Continental shelf, silly, I would say. And what is a sponge? Whale shark, silly, I would say. Tell me about your mother.

Mother?

Mother is tall, thin, bony and very nervous. Her whole body is strung by some high voltage wire that is constantly singing with a thin insect squeak of tension. The muscles in her cheeks bunch into little ridges, and her mouth becomes a thin, red slit in her face.

While Father is a gothic, stained glass window, Mother is the pointed, skeleton structure of a wooden church steeple. Sometimes the inside is empty, and the sunlight shines through cracking, split walls onto the sagging floor in musty, golden bars that pick up the dust as it swirls and hangs in the air. When something from below triggers the metal pistons inside the church, the steeple is suddenly and unexpectedly filled with the wild, uncontrolled clamor of bells, making noise but playing no tune in particular, calling people to church, a ghost church, without knowing why.

Mother has a lot of personality in a scatterbrained, scared way. She is scared of life and lives under a mask of false fierceness, growling at the flowers and tiny stones.

I have rarely seen her smile and more rarely heard her laugh. When she did, it was at the child-antics of my little brother.

Her nervousness is a physical defect as it has taken over her whole life and affected everything she does. Everything is a frantic clutching and clawing to stay within sanity. An upset carries her almost over the rim of the bowl in which swirls the black whirlpool of hysteria. She lives in no-guy's land by herself.

My father stands on the outside of this land, guarding against any possible intruders, but not being able to enter himself as he is an outsider to these complexes and tensions. Caught helplessly in the network of nerves, my mother has turned her two older children against her. I was shivering inside. I was trying to catch her eyes.

I hated her when I was little. She charged me with being afraid and then laughed. You got to eat, you got to drink. She gave me and my sister nothing to grow on, and then was surprised when we did things to show her we didn't love her. She gave us no answers, no explanations for anything and was too embarrassed to tell us about the facts of life. You got to run, you got to hide. She withdrew to the past in her almost maniacal refuge in civil war novels. She became a book herself in the face of our hostility towards her . . . open pages, written on by other people . . . mixed prose and poetry, confused ideas, archaic rules of life laid flat for nobody to read, for they are out of date. But it's so hard, it's really hard. Sometimes I feel like goin' down.

Mother's two virtues are her perseverance and her often unexpected compassion. When one of us is hurt or sick she is a constant, watchful nurse. Since she too has known the pain of childbirth, made worse for her by her nervousness and fear of the unknown, and knows that it is to battle against the very air in order to survive, she is quick to help others who need help. With an eagle eye, she can spot the hypocrite, the hypochondriac, and is sarcastic and often mean to them too harshly as if they were much below her. Oh yes. You can wear a mask and paint your face. You can call yourself the human race. You can wear a collar and a tie. One thing you can't hide is when you're crippled inside.

I will not be pushed around in my own house! And especially by my own children. We will all eat at six o'clock, and no one is to be later. You will make your beds after breakfast and clean your rooms on Saturday morning. The cleanest room will earn a gold star. Her main worry was that we had a habit of leaving our underpants on the floors of our rooms. My father acted as an army inspector. Well now you know that your cat has nine lives babe, nine lives by itself, but you only got one. Mamma take a look outside, please. But she didn't. And so I can never go home again. I can't. I can never go home. And I cannot go home. Mothers are sick people. Sick, sick people, Joe.

'Why did you come back home?' I asked.

'Because I realized that the stakes are myself. I have no other ransom money, nothing to break or barter but my life, my spirit measured out, in bits, spread over the roulette table. I recoup what I can. Nothing else to shove under the nose of the *maître de jeu.* Nothing to thrust out the window, no white flag. This flesh all I have to offer, to make the play with this immediate head, what it comes up with as we slither over this board, stepping always between the lines. Yet I don't envy Savonarola.'

'You're a fool, Joe. Mothers are sick, sick people. And mother Zip will kill you. Did you see the *Call to Arms* on the square?

> *If it takes a*
> *B L O O D B A T H*
> *let's get it over with.*
> *No more*
> *appeasement.*

'My clock, Benedetta, hangs on a wall-hook, directly under a coconut husk, and momentum of the ticking makes it rock back and forth. I'm totally free, now . . .'

'No, Joe. George Jackson already lived and died for the revolution. And the blood in my eye explains why. But you have to run. And fast.'

He smiled. Then said: 'The dark showed me a face. My ghosts are all guys. The light becomes me. Do not fear the day.'

And I: 'For centuries mercy is the howl of the assassinated. And this city has even got the machine that grinds out dreams.'

'Perhaps my words of love are drowned by the thud of the mind. And I know I love in vain, strive against hope. Yet in this captious and untenable sieve I still pour in the water of my love, and lack not to lose still. You must have faith in life, Benedetta. Life is darkly strong.'

'They are waiting for you, Joe. And tomorrow I can write the day of the jackal. For a touch of irony one loses all?'

'Benedetta, I know. I read my history as a night watchman reads the hours of rain. Yet my life has no handles at its doors. I don't prepare myself for death. I know the origin of things. The end is a surface on which journeys the invader of my shadow. I do not know the shadows.'

XXVIII

In the morning they called him from the square. And he went out, all naked, except for his snappy, black and white oxfords with platforms and high heels bought at the JuJu boutique in New York. Only the sheep, my little me, turned round on his way back with ragged head and eyes of salt. Really nothing happens in the world, and man still hangs the rain in his raven wings and cries out love and dissonance. In the flood. Since eternity, we've never lacked for blood.

Zip went over to him, in the public square, and said: 'You've come a long way, baby Joe.'

'Yes, mother.'

'Not yours. Not anymore. I'm a good egg's ass. A good egg, not a cocksman.'

'Yes, you're still a pretty guyster.'

'Well, yes. But you're not going to scare me shitless.'

'No, I won't, because the freakier the shoe, the higher the platform and heel, the better it sells. But listen, in your unlit sexnests boys and girls are getting unhappily, unecstatically, unlovingly fed. Why do you still want a penny for that? I bet you haven't blessed a single chick in need of a Confessor.'

'Who cares? I'm only quick to spot a queer. To kiss my enemies. In fact, between you and me — no understanding. I think in one way, you in another. This is my territory. So why did you come back? To scorn me?'

'You may say I'm a dreamer, but I'm not the only one. I hope someday you'll join us and the word will be as one.'

'You're wrong. Because I know what you want. All you want is to eat something else instead of veal.'

'No, Zip. Give me back Benedetta and all the galls you keep, that's all. We have joined the movement to go back to turn-of-the-century rural living . . .'

'Too late. Rats gleaming with disease come out to spread garbage fever through Jersey City. But our oil spill detectives will take the oil's fingerprints and the culprit will be apprehended. All the Bronx guys will suffer.'

'I do not ask to see the distant scene.'

'You must at last. It's the haggling that does it. Pimple Boy, come on here with the crates . . .'

Pimple Boy went over to them and reached into one of the crates and took out a Sauer 7.66-mm. automatic. He handed this to Zip. Reached in again and brought out a Police Positive .38 revolver. He handed this to Joe. On the third dip he came up with a short-barrelled Smith & Wesson .32 revolver. He handed this to himself. A reason, I suppose, for going along with no fuss. So I knew he was going to be killed. And I screamed, but no one heard it. Joe's band, under the leadership of Fosco Fiaschetti, started playing a beautiful Hymn. Let music for peace be the paradigm. For peace means to change at the right time, as the world clock goes tick and tock. Zip's band replied: 'And it's one, two, three, what are we waiting for? Don't ask me I don't give a damn. The next stop is in your band.'

Joe said: 'These violent delights have violent ends.'

'*L'appetit vient en mangeant*, as they say in France,' said Zip.

'I know, I know that you drink nothing but champagne,' Joe said. 'But you'll drink any kind of champagne that can be poured. I know you've got a boat called the *Pair-o'-dice*, and I was on it when you caught a marlin one time, and I was on it when you let the marlins get away half a dozen times . . .'

'But you're not going to get away. So let me kiss you gently . . .'

'The good man is the builder, if he builds what is good. Unfortunately your beard has grown in straggly and gray, making you look more like a wino on the bum.'

'Getting stir-crazy, huh?'

Zip's voice was yappish, like a terrier's.

Zip felt the heft of the gun in his hand.

'Wait, wait . . .' cried the Fish. 'If this guy Joe dies, they'll probably turn New Jersey upside down. These kind of people . . . it's a pleasure to stay away from them. They are ready to explode at the drop of a hat. They are really touchy. They have a peacemaker in this land.'

No time, no time. The bands started playing again. And then, when the rest had escaped behind the walls of the city, Joe stood without, determined to await the combat. His old father Joseph Adonis called to him from the walls and begged him to retire nor tempt to encounter. His mamma, Venerea, also besought him to the same effect, but all in vain.

'How can I,' Joe said, 'by whose command the people went to his day's contest, where so many have fallen, seek safety for myself against a fake foe?'

'Watch Pimple Boy!' I yelled, in terror.

But he got it. When Zip came within reach of his Sauer 7.66-mm. automatic, he waited the approach of Joe. When he came within reach Pimple Boy aimed his gun at that part where the armor leaves the neck uncovered, and Joe fell, death-wounded, and feebly said: 'Spare my body! Let my parents ransom it, and let me receive funeral rites from the sons and daughters of the Bronx.'

To which Zip replied: 'Insane dog, name not ransom nor pity to me, on whom you have brought such dire distress.'

So the whip was dropped in exhaustion, and I sank on a seat in a kind of lethargic stupor. Because, you see Joe, there exists such a thing as noble defeat.

But soon a riot skirmished out. Pimple Boy was knifed down. By unknown.

'The contest was rigged,' the protesters claimed.

And others said, 'It's time to move on with routine business.'

One red face yelled, 'No question about it. It's a non-acceptable fraud.'

Lights went on with sirens and water pumps. More than 1,000 demonstrators were now fighting a fierce battle in the arena, exchanging tear gas, rocks and gasoline bombs. The fight with a few hundred went on along the streets near a building that housed Zip's groups, and barricades were set up by kids and people with caches of firebombs and rocks.

A crowd gathered on the main streets leading to the capitol building hurling firebombs and rocks, and clashes continued into the night.

The Fish, rather than Fosco Fiaschetti, mumbled the final speech. And he said: 'The weight of this sad time we must obey. Speak what we feel, nor what we ought to say. The youngest hath borne most. We that are the very old shall never see so much.'

Such honours the Bronx to her hero paid
And peaceful slept the mighty Joe's shade.

Oh, hoooooh! Hooooooh! My voice started railing with an ugliness and pain reminiscent to my ear of the wild grunt of a wounded pig. I felt as if I were being despoiled of a vital part of myself, and in the middle of this horror I noted that I screamed like a pig, not a lion, nor a bear.

I went back to the joint. But no, no welcome, no warmth, the warmth that had been through Joe, as if it never had been, like the cancellation that is assumed, with drink, 'Yah well, he punched him in the nose, but he was drunk.' So they were excused, and it didn't really matter. It didn't really happen. Death does not happen. Does it happen?

Oh, hooooo! Hoooooooo!

Death! Hoooooo! Death, death, death! Does it really matter? Death, does it really happen? Death does not happen. Oh, hooooooh! Hoooooooooh!

But here it's sadder. For a moment there's a spark of genuineness, however humble, a spark of the core, the core that loves and wants to be loved. And the core accordingly gives. But now, *Closed*, no entry, no exit.

'I'm sorry, Benedetta,' said the Fish.

'Don't be.'

Once again, they send me a newspaper, upstairs. With the note: *Well, isn't this one your lover?*

JOE ADONIS
CRIME CZAR DIES

ANCONA, Italy — In the United States he was 'Mr. A', a feared figure once described by the late Sen. Estes Kefauver as a chief of a gangland assassination bureau called Murder Inc.

In Italy as an exile in the land of his birth, he was Giuseppe Antonio Doto.

Joe Adonis, 69, one of the last survivors of a ruthless era in American crime when police considered him a partner of Frank Costello, Al Capone, Charles 'Lucky' Luciano and Vito Genovese, died Friday of heart failure and congested lungs in an Ancona hospital room guarded by police. His West German housekeeper sat at his bedside.

Once police called him head of all Brooklyn rackets, an associate of Costello in Florida crime, and one of the bookmakers on the East Coast.

He used an olive oil importing business called 'Mamma Mia Importing Co.' to mask much of his illegal activities, police said. He lived in a mansion with bomb-proof walls. American crime investigators called him one of the most dangerous and astute gangsters in the United States and described him as a chief in 'Murder, Inc.', the enforcement agency of the Mafia.

A lie cost Adonis all that wealth, power and fearful respect.

He told a Kefauver committee investigating organized crime that he was born in Passaic, N.J., but the committee knew he was born in the Italian village of Montemarano near Naples. A gravedigger there remembered him as a poor boy who went to the United States in 1909.

To avoid a five year prison term and deportation for perjury, Adonis returned to Italy on Jan. 15, 1956.

Once back in the homeland he barely remembered, Adonis tried to stay out of the public eye — and succeeded most of the time. Roman authorities ordered him out of the city once, and Neapolitan police once said he was not welcome, but otherwise few Italians knew or cared who he was.

Then on May 22, police removed him from his deluxe apartment in central Milan and detained him until June 20 when a court banished him to a remote hillside village as socially dangerous.

No, no, no, of course. So I started packing. My breasts grew and became sore, and I knew I was pregnant. And I began to put my things in boxes, and pack up the odds and ends of my life.

From a remote distance, the Fish was singing on his banjo something like an invitation to freedom and discovery.

I don't need to go Paris or Tokyo
I don't feel to go Venice or Peking
I just want to travel America
I just want to roam thru America
All I want is to see my America
Riding high on a pony from sea to sea.

Good Fish! In my mind one thing: 'I'm the key. The key turns in the door once and turns once only.'

Then I went downstairs. All these fellows were there, inside, when I entered with my naked skin. They had been drinking, and began to spit on me. And I understood nothing. I was just a mermaid who had lost her way. They pocked me with cigarette ends and with burnt corks, and rolled on the bar floor in raucous laughter. My lips moved soundlessly, and ultimately I left by that door.

The ancient move off on frail bird's feet, upraised, while a runaway surf travels naked in the wind.

Post-Word

Was it good zook? Boy, was I turned on! Is this the truth? Boy, I don't know. I dreamt I was all bones. I only know that once I met a chick by the name of Benedetta. And I only know that once, by reading a poem of love, I said to her, in the cockpit of my airplane: 'I wish I could remember how to forget this pain about not being able to remember the past before meeting you.'

She was a Beautiful Person, an enigmatic femme fatale. No man who was seeking to know how the wind blows could afford to ignore Benedetta, the intellectual's pinup. And she was good at manipulating the very rich and the very famous. She was a mirror that gave a man back the image of himself he wanted to see. She had a social-climbing sex appeal. She believed in things and she was motivated by her beliefs. But she was not collecting real estate. Sex, in fact, for her was neutral, like money. It's the way you use it that counts. And she used it in the way she wanted. Only later, when she vanished from someone's life, they sadly discovered she wasn't anyone's exclusive property. And I also felt that she was on temporary loan. But yes, I loved her, uh!

I was an uptown Bohemian, you know. I had a disturbed life: three days in New York chez Madison, and three days in California, with the grape workers, the fighting Chicanos, drinking Pernod. And one first time she said to me, 'Chauvinist.' She came to New York for the weekend. Someone was playing the piano and she did a tap dance. She was a helluva dancer. And to her I said, 'You've come a long way, baby Benedetta.'

She said, 'Chauvinist!'

That Sunday I rented a plane and flew her back to her college among the mountains of Appalachia. She was still in college, the Anabasis College, and I was still with one foot in New York and the other one in California. I used to visit her on weekends. I'd rent a plane in Los Angeles and fly over her dormitory and write her name in the sky. I always had trouble crossing the two *t*'s.

I introduced her to many people, the right people. Then she started sending me strange letters, one talking about Lucretia Mott and Charlotte Perkins Gilman and Eleanor Roosevelt, and one spelling out with fury that men insist that all they need is a good lay and then they'll be straight, and that the average man can't bear to think that a woman might prefer another woman to him, and he's threatened by a woman who obviously chooses to live without a man.

But she also sent me letters like this: . . . *god knows I've thought and rethought about you since you flashed again to New York — so fast I hardly got a good look at you. You know that those tears you always inspire in me are very angry ones; anger at the frustration that I've been living with for too long — and you, who I've known in snatches and in some ways so fully, for whom I want to soar, sing and laugh, you're so definitely important to me, that when you catch me with my pants down I snarl and the tears eventually win. If I could sit calmly beside a screaming truth without budging, I wouldn't want to know myself . . .*

When, one day in November, she sent me a post card of love from New Jersey, by signing it *Benedetta in Guysterland*, I did not know what she was up to, nor what she meant.

She received a Wassermann test from someone recovering from hepatitis. And she became psychotic after a benign cyst had been removed from her vulva. From common friends I learned, later, that she spent much of her time smoking and discussing ultra-modern views of sex with sophisticated spinsters. And two months after the operation on her vulva she became excited, said the doctor had aroused her sexually and that he had robbed her of her sex. She was greatly upset when this physician

mentioned the possibility of an early meno-
pause. She walked about her house nude and
frequently said, 'I have to know the truth; is
there something wrong with me?' While still
under the influence of an overdose of allonal
which she had taken with suicidal intent, she
said, 'I am still in the dark as to sex; there are
two sides to me: my male side and my female
side. I must have relations with a man and a
woman — must have sexual experience — I
must have a full term baby. Sex has been hidden from me.'

She exposed herself to her doctor, in-
dulged in autoerotic practices with him,
entered a neighbor's home and offered herself
to two men there, saying that she was the sister
of Mozart. She pursued a sixteen-year-old
neighbor lad with such zeal that for two weeks
he was afraid to leave his home. On the day
before admission to the hospital, it was a problem to keep her from assaulting men.

I never believed she was what people said
she had become, not even after her marvelous
disintegration in the crystal clear water in the
guy village of Cherry Grove. Yet we seemed to
be divided by some shade, always. I was re-
peating to myself: 'I must lose myself in action,
lest I wither in despair.' At night, before blowing out the lantern, I formed the habit of block-
ing out the morrow's work. It was a case of
assigning myself an hour to leveling drift, an
hour to straightening up the fuel drums, an

hour to cutting bookshelves in the walls of the food tunnel, and two hours to renewing a broken bridge in the nasal passage.

I didn't have a problem, because a problem well-stated is a problem half-solved. But I wanted to tell her story, and I did not know how. I never wrote in English before. But somebody from the hill was screaming at me: 'For God's sake, get babies out of the laboratory and back in the womb where they belong.' So I understood I could write a story about Benedetta, and I started driving a '33 Ford with a gallon jar on the hood for a gas tank. I didn't butt my head against a wall like a rat in a maze. Nor did I go to serve a rap for income tax evasion, because I do pay taxes. So I wrote the story.

When the space between the trees was getting dimmer, I started patching together words and words, and after a while the light gleamed on polished mahogany and brass, on rich flooring and rich woodwork, on muted oil paintings and shelves of lost books. A picture on the wall reminded me of a man part sadist, part con man, part dreamer. He could have been a spellbinding talker, pleasant to be around for a while. But, then, I left, leaving the house ablaze with light. No shadow between my name and the tides. I went out in the open and read, on a billboard: *As traffic gets worse, outdoor advertising gets better.* True. So, I thought, allow the wise poet to strive to be modest in his lines. And I walked away.

Let's hope there's no monsoon Thursday.

Appendix

Benedetta and Environs

1. The Readers

I've been circulating for years the manuscript *Benedetta* among friends. Their names:

Eugene Mirabelli, novelist; Dorothy Harrison, Lecturer in English, State University of New York at Albany; Ada Hinshaw, graduate student; Paul Pimsleur, Professor of Education and Romance Languages, State University of New York at Albany; David C. Redding, Associate Professor of English, State University of New York at Albany; Edwin C. Munro, Professor of Spanish, State University of New York at Albany; Jean Paris, literary critic, Professor of Romance Languages, John Hopkins University; Lowry Nelson, Jr., Professor of Comparative Literature, Yale University; Luigi Ballerini, poet, Assistant Professor of Italian, City College, New York; William O. Perlmutter, Professor of Sociology, former Dean of the Arts and Sciences College, State University of New York at Albany; Silvana Cohen, short-story writer; P.M. Pasinetti, novelist; Giovanni Cecchetti, Professor of Italian, University of California at Los Angeles; Franco Betti, Assistant Professor of Italian, University of California at Los Angeles; Leslie A. Fiedler, literary critic, Professor of English, State University of New York at Buffalo; John di Palma, real estate agent; Ms. Laraine Rowe, secretary.

This list goes back to 1971-72, the time of the following notes.

2. The Questions

Not all of *Benedetta's* readers wrote a report about the book. They told me verbally, *de visu*, or by phone, their opinions. Those who wrote a report, however, expressed the desire to know both the readers' reactions and my reaction to the reactions. I have no reactions. In fact, I sympathize with all the reports.

A few readers asked: 'Is this a book about Mafia?' 'Is this a book about Homosexuals?' 'Is this a book about Women's Liberation?' 'Is this a book about Pornography?' 'Is this a book about Literature?' 'Is this a Satire, a Prose-Poem, a Collage?'

A collage for sure. And, as for the other questions, I don't know if I know. This is why I asked for a report. Though knowing that I know every line of the book, its composition, the end-result that I hoped to achieve, still let the others tell me what it is all about.

This is a research book. In literature, a research book is a critical book most of the time. Never a novel, however. Instead I wanted to do a novel based on research, hence on language. I wanted to tease my mind. I wanted to tease your mind. I can't say therefore, like Flaubert, *'Madame Bovary c'est moi.'* This *Benedetta* is a worldly creature. We all contributed to her creation. A kind of universal soul through which we may or may not recover knowledge. Being a writer in a new land, it happened that I was in a particular need of that recovery. So *Benedetta* slept with me more than with you, giving

214

me a hope that Leslie Fiedler has articulated in this nice way: '. . . I think it would be a great loss to all of us if you did not become an American novelist at this point.'

3. The Bibliography

One reader said: 'Why are you fishing that way? I recognized a line from Montale . . .' Another said: 'Why are you fishing that way? I recognized a line from Shakespeare . . .' Yet another interrogated: 'Really, why are you fishing that way? From whom do you quote? Do you have a bibliography? The silver fish ran in and out of your special bindings . . .'

My readers read the book at a time when the Irving 'autobiography' was making headlines. They could also have asked: 'What have you done to us?' But they didn't say it. They knew that my clock goes round and round, and centuries creak on my back. It was a miracle, for me, to be able to listen for long hours to the voice of Roethke, and when the silence again came I could utter, 'dust in a corner stirred, and the walls stretched wide, as I went fishing my way, my way,' fishing Donne, fishing Stephen Crane, fishing Homer and W.H. Auden, Leopardi and Germaine Greer and T.S. Eliot, Coleridge and Martha Mitchell, Swift and Tom Wolfe, Dante and Anthony Burgess, Shelley and Norman Mailer, Henry James and Che Guevara, Marvell and Pablo Neruda, Alexander Pope and Horace, Joyce with Blake, Robert Herrick with *The New York Times* and *Vogue*, underground newspapers and *Esquire*, as I went fishing my way, my way.

However, if you want to trace down the main sources, move about the following: Shakespeare's plays, sonnets, and *Venus and Adonis*; *The De Cavalcante Tapes*, released by the FBI, June 10, 1969; *Honor Thy Father*, by Gay Talese, New York, 1971; *The Varieties of Psychedelic Experience*, by Masters and Houston, New York, 1966; *The Homosexuals*, edited by A.M. Krick, New York, 1964; *Memoirs of a Beatnik*, by Diane di Prima, New York, 1969; *The Movement Toward a New America*, assembled by Mitchell Goodman, New York, 1970; *Words for the Wind*, by Theodore Roethke, Bloomington, Indiana, 1961; *The Parable of Peanuts*, by Robert L. Short, New York, 1968; *The Pearl*, New York, 1968; *Fille de joie*, New York, 1967; *Selected Poems*, Eugenio Montale, New York, 1965; *The Selected Writings of Salvatore Quasimodo*, New York, 1960; *We Are Many*, Pablo Neruda, London, 1970; *Currents*, by Thomas Sanders, Beverly Hills, California, 1971; *The Woman as Nigger*, by Jane Gallion, Canoga Park, California, 1970; *White Racism: a Psychohistory*, by Joel Kovel, New York, 1971; *The Performing Self*, by Richard Poirier, Boston, Massachussets, 1971; *Esquire Magazine*, September, October, 1971; 'Fag Rag', Fall 1971, Boston, Massachussets; Giose Rimanelli's *Polypidom Pink* (unedited poems); John Lennon's *Plastic Ono Band* (Stereo SW 3372), and *Imagine* (Stereo SW 3379); James Taylor's *Sweet Baby James* (Stereo SW 1843); Country Joe McDonald's *Woodstock* (Stereo SD 3-500).

4. The Quotations

The fishing business, however, having something to do with a rod and a hook, can only be explained by the way of quotation marks, that is in the way scholars usually imprison in their bindings small and big passages taken from other books.

As an example of reeling in from the best side of the word's pond, I shall examine the structure of the first Chapter of *Benedetta*.

'I love you,'[1] Joe Adonis. 'While I'll wind the wild-woods' bluckbells among my window's weeds,'[2] Your Benedetta,[3] indeed — 'a former drag

---

1. The first draft of *Benedetta* was called 'Lady Mmmm' and sent to Jean Paris in Paris. 'I love you' was written in Old English, 'Ic e lufie.'

2. James Joyce's *Finnegans Wake*, note 1, p. 282, Viking Compass Edition, 1967.

3. The name Benedetta was first suggested by the proverb, '*San Benedetto una rondine sotto il tetto*', which indicates the first day of spring, March 20, when the swallows reappear on our roofs. I was reappearing to life after a car accident, and for me it was spring again. The name Benedetta, however, was also that of Benedetta Marinetti, wife of F.T. Marinetti, poet, the founder of a literary movement called Futurismo, with a manifesto published on the Parisian *Figaro*, February 22, 1909. Benedetta is also the name of a lady whom I never met, Benedetta Barzini, daughter of the Italian journalist and writer, Luigi Barzini. The young American poet Gerard Malanga wrote for her lovely poems, and once, in New York, he took me to the screening of a short film that he had just made for her. My Benedetta, however, has no connection with either Benedetta Marinetti or Benedetta Barzini. Two girls are behind Benedetta's sensibility: Jane and Phoebe, who loved me dearly. On the literary level, however, I was thinking first about Milly, daughter of Molly, in Joyce's *Ulysses*; and second, about the fate of Madame de Stael's *Corinne*.

star on the word stage,'[4] now playing 'public sexophone'[5] with *The Untouchable*[6] *Seven Sages*. 'All the world's a stage,'[7] you know, 'and all the men and women merely players. They have their exits and their entrances,'[8] yet only 'one man in' this 'time plays many parts,'[9] and his name is Santo 'Zip the Thunder' Tristano,[10] always 'sudden and quick in

---

4. A line read on an underground newspaper, *Georgia Straight*, published in Vancouver, Canada, probably in one of the October issues, 1970. The line was: '. . . a former drag star on the world stage.'

5. The word *sexophone* was first used by the Italian writer Curzio Malaparte in a show that had its premiere in the Sistina Theater of Rome, in the mid-fifties. References to it can be found in Luigi Barzini's book, *From Caesar to Mafia*, New York, 1971, pp. 48-60.

6. The title of a TV show about organized crime during the Prohibition era in the United States.

7. Seven Sages is a pun on Shakespeare's Seven Ages, in *As You Like It*, Scene VII:

'All the world's a stage,
And all the men and women merely players;
They have their exits and their entrances,
And one man in his time plays many parts,
His acting being seven ages.'

8. In *As You Like It*, edited by Albert Gilman, Signet Classic Shakespeare, New York, 1963, see lines 140-141.

9. *Ibid*. The substitution of *his* with *this*.

10. Santo 'Zip the Thunder' Tristano. The name Santo came first to my mind by association with the name Sante, Sante Monachesi, an Italian painter with whom I had a friendly relationship for over twenty years. Zip the Thunder was suggested by 'Sam the Plumber' DeCavalcante, a Cosa Nostra boss from New Jersey whose office was 'bugged' by the FBI, and the DeCavalcante Tapes were made public on June 10, 1969. Tristano, instead, comes directly from Joyce's *FW*, 'Sir Tristram, violer d'amores, fr'over the short sea, had pass-encore rearrived from North Armorica on this side the scraggyisthmus of Europe Minor to wielderfight his penisolate war . . .'

quarrel, seeking the bubble reputation.'[11] But 'you
still shine from here,'[12] Joe, 'for I am forever peering'[13] over the Jersey territory 'at you, still mirthing
with you, grappling, double back beasting it with
you.'[14] And 'it can't be otherwise.'[15] 'We did sleep
days out of countenance and made the night light
with loving,'[16] 'till it was soaring.'[17] 'It is so long,
the spring which goes on all winter. Time lost its
shoes. A year is four centuries.'[18] 'When I sleep
every night, what am I called or not called? And
when I wake, who am I if I was not I while I slept?'[19]
'This means to say that scarcely have we landed into
life than we come as if newborn.'[20] 'I have a mind

11. *As You Like It*, edition already quoted, lines 151-152.

12. From a private love letter by J.F.

13. *Ibid.*

14. *Ibid.*

15. From a night-night show on TV.

16. *Antony and Cleopatra*, Act II, Scene II, line 181.

17. J.F., letters.

18. Pablo Neruda's 'Too Many Names', from *We Are Many*, translated by Alastair Reid, London, 1970:

Es tan larga la primavera
que dura todo el invierno:
el tiempo perdia los zapatos:
un año tiene cuatro siglos.

19. *Ibid.*

Cuando duermo todas las noches,
como me llamo o no me llamo?
Y cuando me despierto quien soy
si no era yo cuando dormia?

20. *Ibid.*

Esto quiere decir que apenas
desembarcamos en la vida,
que venimos recièn naciendo.

to confuse things.'[21] Yet, 'the only thing that troubles me'[22] is why they send you into exile, 'Without a smile.'[23]

'The way people carry on you'd think there was something wrong.'[24] And so 'you have been busted,'[25] and 'you can't begin to understand the reason,'[26] 'with so many faltering names, with so many sad formalities, with so many pompous letters, with so much as yours and mine, with so much signing of papers.'[27] But 'I have no wish to change my planet.'[28] I just need 'one young surgeon'[29] or a 'pretty Mister Professor to make up time,'[30] and the loss of you 'in sharing nonsenses.'[31]

'She's beautiful and powerful and knows what's

---

21. *Ibid.*

Y pienso confundir las cosas.

22. J.F., letters.

23. An advertisement from a fashion magazine.

24. From a talk show on TV, probably Dick Cavett.

25. From a show on Lenny Bruce.

26. *Ibid.*

27. Pablo Neruda's already quoted *Too Many Names*:

con tantos nombres inseguros,
con tantas etiquetas tristes,
con tantas letras rimbombantes,
con tanto tuyo y tanto mio,
con tanta firma en los papeles.

28. Pablo Neruda's 'Lazybones', from *We Are Many*, already quoted:

No quiero cambiar de planeta.

29. From a TV show, probably *Ben Casey*.

30. From a novel published by a woman's magazine, probably *Cosmopolitan.*

31. *Ibid.*

right for all mankind. Anytime,'[32] they say. 'They never got married and lived happily ever after,'[33] because Joe Adonis — in his 'crusade for sexual liberation — was beating a dead horse.'[34] But 'this isn't true,'[35] since 'women are far more sensitive than men to musk-like odors derived from substances whose chemical structures are similar to that of testosterone, the male sex hormone.'[36] There is instead 'something to cheer about in the ever-increasing use of perfumes that have bases derived from animal sex glands, such as ambergris, civet, and musk — which means testicles in Sanskrit.'[37] However, 'the menstrual cycles of coeds living in close proximity with one another tend to become synchronized'[38] and 'this is the trouble'[39] you know, 'because I still don't understand what gay feminism is,'[40] and 'what a radical chic party is,'[41] though I understand why these people around me want to show off with 'their Pucci dresses, Gucci shoes, Capucci scarves;'[42] 'with Elmer's Glue on their oh-so-falsely-Guy eyes, their cockette eyes,

32. From an article by Leonard Levitt about Gloria Steinem, *Esquire*, Vol. LXXVI No. 4, October 1971.

33. *Ibid*.

34. *Ibid*.

35. A TV show, probably *Ironside*.

36. From an article by David M. Rorvik titled 'Present Shock', *Esquire*, Vol. LXXVI No. 4, October, 1971.

37. *Ibid*.

38. *Ibid*.

39. From *Fag Rag*, Fall 1971, Boston, Massachusetts, No. 2.

40. *Ibid*.

41. *Ibid*.

42. *Ibid*.

their Clarabelle eyes, their queen-mocking eyes;'[43] 'With tiny fishes played over their chest'; and a 'Colt .38 with bullets six'[44] hung on their back. And 'in the shadow of this stone I do not rest.'[45] So, 'don't call me oversentimental,'[46] Joe. 'I shall continue to drink of you'[47] in this 'stripped, geometrical pied-en-ciel'[48] where Zip the Thunder and his Band keep me as prisoner. 'Do you read me?'[49] 'I never felt my voice so clear, never have been so rich in kisses.'[50] And 'now, as always, it is early. The shifting light is a swarm of bees.'[51]

The longest quotations, ranging from one to three pages, are from Guy Talese's book *Honor Thy Father*, from *The Varieties of Psychedelic Experience*, by Masters and Houston, and from *The Homosexuals*, edited by A. M. Krick.

These quotations, however, have a special

43. *Ibid.*

44. Graham Greene's *The Power and the Glory*, London, Heinemann, 1940, p. 163 and p. 58.

45. Pablo Neruda's 'Nothing More', from *We Are Many*, already quoted:

junto a esta piedra no reposo.

46. From a night-night show on TV.

47. J.F., letters.

48. From a fashion magazine, probably *Vogue*.

49. From U.S.A. military jargon.

50. Pablo Neruda's 'I Ask for Silence', from *We Are Many*, already quoted:

Nunca me sentí tan sonoro,
nunca he tenido tantos besos.

51. *Ibid.*

Ahora, como siempre, es temprano.
Vuela la luz con sus abejas.

flavor: I changed their meaning by way of changing their proposition. I am grateful to their authors for they gave me important material on which to expand my fable.

Another subject, of which I didn't say a thing yet, is the famed Joe Adonis, easily recognizable by the readers as a known underworld figure.

When I started writing *Benedetta*, a piece in *The New York Times* reminded me of a man who was having troubles with the Italian authorities in Milan. That man was saying: 'I'm a sick man. If you send me to exile, it'll kill me.' I chose that name, however, for two reasons: 1) the name Joe is a classical G.I. name. Germaine Greer called Norman Mailer 'Joe Mailer', in reference to G.I. Joe. There was also a film that disturbed me, called *Joe*. 2) Adonis is the god of love in Greek mythology. It happened to be that the man saying in Milan, 'If you send me to exile, it'll kill me', was a famed gangster. Now you know how my mind works: emotions, emotions, emotions, controlled by a larger understanding of myth.

5. Why *Esquire*?

Another question: 'Why did you dedicate the book to a magazine?' ('I never am bored, however familiar the scene.')

I learned English from *Esquire*. An Italian anti-Fascist thinker, who died in prison a long time ago, once told his children that the best way to learn a foreign language is to start translating it, word by word, with the help of a dictionary. That man was Antonio Gramsci. I welcomed the suggestion, and when I turned around *Esquire* mag was near at hand. It happened many years ago in Italy, on a crowded beach after the war. For years I exercised by translating bits of articles from that magazine.

6. Why Bother Writing?

For the difficulty of it, I guess. And the fun of it. Writing as play may also mean writing as a source of life style.

I've been reading printed pages from the age of three, and I've been writing from the age of nine. I guess because I was alone. After a while I started piling manuscripts on the shelves of my bathroom where I often work. A dozen of these manuscripts just got out of hand, when I thought I was a writer and when I knew I needed money. And they worked their way up publishers' winding staircases, eventually reaching bookstore glass windows.

Once I wrote myself a tiny poem. It goes this way:

when I looked in the mirror
later in the morning
and saw no reflection
I knew something was wrong:

life
a strange sideways-aware
bleakness

and yet
even if things are to fail
I must make the attempt
anyway.

One day in my life I thought that literature is nothing but a burning hatred for one's own insecurity, and a wish to be free of that self-hatred. And another day I thought that literature is people, education, fancy and fantasy, winter and summer, cold hands. A disease of the brain.

Now I don't think too much about it. I just go on, as always. Writing.

7. A Mad, Obsessed Book

Here are the reports in the order of their arrival. The first one, undated, is by Eugene Mirabelli, a Harvard Ph.D., a Viking novelist, a shy man with a pale smile who fears high buildings, and most of the time looks for unwanted listeners behind his shoulders.

Benedetta in Guysterland is a mad, obsessed book — a poet's nightmare. It is a novel in which the words have taken over and are running things. 'This time,' says Rimanelli in his For-a-word, 'I only wished to be a free collector of paper joy and paper anguish instead of a producer of them — in order to attempt a new experiment on verbs and syntax, speech, writing, and paranoia... My body was covered with sentences, words, newspaper print. Then I took a shower.' *Benedetta* is the liquid novel run-off. It is a fantastic braiding together of sentences into a design which shifts and alters as we look at it, a kaleidoscope which changes at the slightest nudge. To read this novel is to recapture the disoriented shock which was felt by those reviewers of fifty years ago who saw Picasso's new paintings with fresh eyes.

8. High Comedy

The second, undated, is by Dorothy Harrison, an excellent tennis player, mother of one, smiling face, pretty as a Van Gogh sunflower.

Giose Rimanelli caresses the underside of the underword, under-world, under-wear(where), in his liquid novel *B. in G.* Breaking down the barriers of sex and art, he merges Here Comes Every Artist with Anna Livia Plurabelle. By drawing on the works of many separate writers, some professional and some not, he confirms the power of language as the unifier and creator of all experience and, ultimately, of reality. *B.in G.* is the final metamorphosis of the world into word. It shows the poet's power to change the word-world, the power of love and death, of kiss and kill. To deny the author the right to make his work from any and all other works is to affirm the separateness of man. By assuming a female narrator as the voice which speaks for him and for all of us, Giose, on one level, asserts the unity of the sexes as well as the unity of all artists. Finally, the book is high comedy. It may well be the divine and cosmic pun which unriddles our existence.

9. A Valuable Valuelessness

The third, undated, is by Ada Hinshaw, student-married, cool majesty, drives a Morgan, sometimes an Opel, at home wears dark eyeglasses. We took classical guitar lessons together.

Others will say things about your book as book,

Giose, but I want to say something about your book as Giose. Because this time you've really done it — you've worded the world of calicocrazy that for you is a way of life. For a long time now I've watched as you watch things falling away from the center and laughed at the spectacle with your sexy roar. I've watched as you transmogrify all values to a valuable valuelessness and build up a Giosean unity from ununity. And I've watched you refusing to believe anything unless you feel like it. And believing anything when you feel like it. (I remember your inserting yourself with cocktail into a discussion about Rousseau (Jean-Jacques) and talking forty-five minutes about Rousseau (Douanier). When at last the misunderstanding was realized, you said it didn't matter — all that you'd said held true for their Rousseau too.) It doesn't do any good to ask if you're serious. Of course you're serious. And your book is serious. It's serious in its reduction of externals to nonsense in order to build up a new sense. It's serious in its exuberant acceptance of the unholding center. And, most of all, it's serious in its unique reassociation of a long dissociated sensibility.

I hope your book has a gold lamé cover.

10. I Hate the Guyster Notion

The fourth, dated November 8th, 2 a.m., is by Paul Pimsleur, author of language books, and co-author of mine in the children's book Poems Make Pictures (Pantheon, 1972), a New Yorker, entrepreneur, lover of photography, films, food, and transcendental meditation.

Your book, *Benedetta in Guysterland*, is surely going to be a hit, and I am going to feel a fool when you become the cynosure of critical attention for the very things I've criticized about it. But you asked me to, so here goes.

You have such a talent for straight narrative, Giose, that I wish you would not complicate the story-telling by introducing literary games. I am interested in the PEOPLE in your book — the heroine above all, but also her father (the best-drawn character in the book, for me). I would like to know them better than you allow me to, and I don't have any concern to know Joe or Willie, who are not characters at all but just names.

Nor do I want to play at identifying quotations from here and there. You are educated. I am educated, we are all educated. We know a lot of quotes, but it doesn't help us live smarter or wiser. You run the risk of distancing potential readers by intellectual one-upmanship, while not winning over to your side anyone worth having there.

I hate the 'guyster' notion. It is insulting, since it takes the part of society's most retrograde attitudes (which are fast disappearing, by the way). And it adds no insight into your characters.

Giose, I think you try to do too much in a single work and that you ought to separate your genres and do one at a time. I've already said which I'd like to see you do. I want to read the straightforward novel about real people that you obviously have in you to write. But I have a hunch that you will have to break away from academia to write it. You are too involved in addressing literary colleagues (a pejorative term in my vocabulary) and not enough involved in talking to walk-around-people.

Now tell me I have missed the point — as undoubtedly I have, since there is so much in the book I simply couldn't understand. But if there is a point, and if I've missed it, it has got to be a little bit the writer's fault as well as mine.

Have you thought of combing files of old photographs of gangsters, molls, etc. for illustrations? Or camping it up with pictures à la Bonnie & Clyde?

The Post-word, by the way, is very moving, very touching — again because it lets us in on the personality of a real person — a person of whom we can be very fond — you.

11. A Basic Metaphor

The fifth, dated November 9, 1971, is by David C. Redding, a student's friend, smokes homemade cigarettes, brings his homemade lunch to his office, at night sleeps in a house full of children.

I have read the typescript of your novel *Benedetta in Guysterland*, and my general reaction is one of great approval and even enthusiasm.

I am particularly impressed by your basic idea — the use of quotations in the way that painters have made collages and sculptors have made assemblages from found objects. Your book is one of the most successful attempts I know of to apply a technique or concept developed by one branch of the arts to another (although that statement seems to give too little credit to Joyce and other literary experimenters).

Your basic metaphor, 'the world is gay', seems

to me to work most of the time, but sometimes it was hard for me to go beyond the usual slang connotations of the word 'guy', particularly when the word was used in close proximity to 'transvestite' (which I take to mean, among other things, a gangster). The punning metaphor of 'band', I thought, was completely successful, and the 'kill-kiss' worked particularly well because of its connection not only with 'guy bands' but with the kiss of death.

I find it remarkable that you were able to vary the style of the book as much as you did. That is, some sections have a somewhat zany quality while others, such as the section on the Nabokov County man seem conventional and highly ordered.

Thank you for letting me read it.

12. This Novel Is About Language

The sixth, dated November 12, 1971, is by Jean Paris, author of books on Shakespeare, Rabelais, Joyce, co-founder of the French literary magazine Change. Women love him, he loves women, especially the music of Alice Coltrane.

Giose Rimanelli's *Benedetta in Guysterland* is probably one of the strangest novels I ever read. Apparently its main purpose is satirical, and it is certainly from this point of view that many chapters should be interpreted. For instance: the amazing description of the *Untouchable Seven Sages'* musical activities, their obvious links with the Mafia, the enigmatic dialogues, the erotic scenes, etc. One of the distinct features of this comic dimension is the constant parody of such authors as Blake, Shakespeare, Henry Miller, Joyce, and so on, and the ironic

230

use of quotations. Altogether, any reader might very well regard the entire book as a modern counterpart of a *Bildungsroman*, the epic story of young Benedetta, from her Nabokov County childhood to her final disappearance in a lunatic asylum. But the episodes are so fantastic. The whole pattern is so filled with deliberate contradictions, inconsistencies, impossibilities, that one wonders whether the characters should really be regarded in a naturalistic perspective, or whether the entire book would not simply be about literature. Its very title is already a nest of allusions: Benedetta, to Beatrice and Saint Bernadette (an obvious opposite of the little whore whose orgies are depicted so vividly). Guysterland refers to Rabelais' Gaster episode (the monstrous meals being translated, here, into those wonderful sex scenes). The connection between a young girl and a strange land, as well as its tortured logics and oneiric quality, suggest a symbolic imitation of *Alice in Wonderland*, while 'Gaste' (French adjective for 'waste') may also refer to T.S. Eliot's *The Waste Land*, etc.

This novel is about language. By this I mean that its content is strictly determined by its formal structure and style. It opens with a sentence 'I love you, Joe Adonis', which gradually develops into its own contradictions and finally shapes the whole finality of the 'story'. Several versions will, in fact, coincide, as to Joe Adonis' personality, age, career, escape or death. Did he reach the Garden (which Garden, by the way?) or was he shot by his suspicious accomplices? Everything, here, is rooted in ambiguity — and if there is one thing that Rimanelli's fiction helps us understand, it is that language never communicates anything we could rely on once and for all. The very substance of the lexicon is, here, a deliberate trap. How are we going to understand, that is interpret the constant references to 'guy' instead of 'gay', 'kiss' instead of 'kill', and so on? In his previous novel, *La macchina paranoica* (of which one chapter, 'Opera Buffa', is going to be published this winter in French translation in a new literary magazine, *Change*) Rimanelli has used another medium to convey this self-contradictory character of language: the whole book was based on a systematic distortion of words, reminiscent of *Finnegans Wake*, which succeeded in suggesting five or six different meanings in a sentence. But, here, in *Benedetta* the device is even more crafty, cunning, and puzzling: by writing apparently in a normal, traditional idiom, namely 20th century American, Rimanelli manages to undermine the substance of each word, namely its signification. We are never sure that the sentence we read is the right one. Since a simple transference of two or three letters would radically alter its purpose, and so, literally we wander in a maze. After the experimental French 'new novel' this wonderful new technique of *écriture* will certainly put Giose Rimanelli among the most daring explorers of the modern possibilities (or impossibilities) of literature.

This does not exclude, of course, the quality of some very poetical or very witty passages. The description of life in a Nabokov County village, of Benedetta's father, of Anabasis College, etc. are real jewels, worthy of being quoted in anthologies of contemporary prose. But, as a whole, in spite of its parodic element, this novel leaves a Gitter feeling, a painful impression of anxiety, helplessness and despair. Its uncanny mixture of incompatible genres, its quick shifting from poetry to pornography, from sense to nonsense, from love to atrocity, its discontinuity, its polyphonic structure which gives voice to almost all tendencies of human nature. All these ingredients work wonderfully well, through the craft and mastery of the author. Already a noted artist in the field of fiction, thanks to such novels as *A Social Position*, *Original Sin*, *The Day of the Lion* and so forth, Rimanelli had the uncommon courage to break with all his past devices, formulas and aesthetics, and to venture splendidly in an experiment of which, after his *Macchina*, *Benedetta* is today the most brilliant example.

13. An Experimental Novel

The seventh, dated November 14, 1971, is by Clair Munro, a restrained, soft, warm man with pungent eyes. Wears a goatee, smiles only to friends, talks slowly, suffers intense asthma. The best adviser for students.

I'm just emerging from a fascinated reading of *Benedetta in Guysterland*. The very least one could say of it is that it is a fantastic tour de force. The only comparison I can think of is to those old-fashioned woven rags made from strips and patches of old clothing in every imaginable color. Some of them were works of art, and so is your book.

It seems incredible that snatches and snippets of old prose and verse could be put together in this way to create a novel, but you have done it, and well. This is truly an experimental novel.

It is rarely that a writer to whom English is foreign can get the feel and texture of the language sufficiently to write in it. I mean write, not make compositions. I can only think of Joseph Conrad and Nabokov. But this is a real novel, and no one could have put these parts together who didn't know how to write English. It takes genuine mastery to play with the language, and now and then there is a suggestion of Lewis Carroll.

In ironic fashion, like Appalachia itself, you have brought together the old Puritan Appalachia as it has become, and the newer power and money-hungry immigrants (here the Mafia) to form — what? They are both nicely satirized.

The many ambiguities throughout the book develop a kind of tension that alternates with relaxation. They also permit the development of a unity that nevertheless keeps unraveling.

The first person narrative also gives it unity, but, that too is ambiguous at times. Sex and philosophizing and a sort of Romantic self-viewing are intermingled in a fashion that suggests Rabelais.

I have a feeling that in this novel you are beginning to reveal some of the mysteries of language and creativity. How can parts from so many sources — parts that are bits of an old unity — be put together to make a new unity entirely different from any of the old? From an artistic point of view, you are doing something similar to what Noam Chomsky and Roman Jakobsen seem to have been doing more scientifically.

I have enjoyed it very much.

14. A Bizarre Work

The eighth, dated 15-xi-71, is by Lowry Nelson, bachelor, wears J. Press suits, plays piano for him-

self, reads and speaks currently five languages,
after dinner smokes slender sweet cigars.

This is a remarkably ingenious and bizarre work that deserves to be published for the parodistic montage it is. The tilted words and crazy quilt of quotations run up and down the gamut of English as perhaps the only possible way of parodying James Joyce, the great parodist himself. The only thing like it that I know is a novel published about ten years ago by Lucy Block called the *Hills of Beverly* which renders the greed and vulgarity of Hollywood movie men in the language of the Duc de Saint-Simon. It also brings to mind the novel of Marc Saporta in the form of playing cards to be continually shuffled and reread. Yet this novel has a kind of pathos and dignity in being the uncensored heroizing of the commonplace, a farrago of dream-thought in a distanced but tender vein, and a weird authenticity of aspiration. I would very much like to read it again in its proper medium-print.

P.S. Giose, è strano l'effetto che produce il tuo libro: un misto tra l'irrealtà e l'espressionismo; uno stato di irrequietudine in cui uno non sa cosa avverrà svoltando la pagina, come l'angolo di una città sconosciuta.

15. Language

The ninth, dated early January, 1972, is by Luigi Ballerini, translator of Charles Olson and William Carlos Williams into Italian, author of a book of poems, E. Wears gentle gold-rimmed glasses, combed long blond hair, talks fast, thinks

fast, writes with precision, no mistakes allowed,
builds with his own hands mysterious big boxes
into which he crawls with his child.

. . . Because Adonais is fertility and the book accounts for a wondrous journey: starting from the Rig-Vedas ending in the Waste Land. How? Here is the first part of the story, my story about your book. There used to be, once upon a time, that is, some fertility gods: Tammuz, Adonais, Attis (he who smells Jesse Weston, he is G.D. right) who traveled in the imagination and in the blood of men, reached the most variegated parts of the universe and were brought back (by the imagination and through the blood of other men) to the conscience of Medieval Europe in order to demonstrate either one or both of the following things: 1) Original Christianity was a great deal hotter than contemporary Christian positivism, 2) Christianity sapped the paganism and then evolved towards death. (The two things might even be one and the same thing.) Yes, you know, from the Grail legends to T.S.Eliot. It's pretty sad. But, there is the heart of *Waste Land* (and remember Gatsby, by the way) you stand hand in hand with Bill Williams, and that makes the difference. This difference: LANGUAGE: American (=learnt from — says W. — from Polish grandmothers). Which is like saying that your book is not apology (disguised as humor, romantic touches etc. — even though it may contain all this), your book is primarily the recovery (rather than the rediscovery) of a lost Atlantis. The Atlantis which is even geographically located between EUROPE (Mediterranean Europe, 'where all the legends were borne') and AMERICA, an ATLANTIS OF THE MIND, the

236

Atlantis that, mind you, also sustains the weight of the world (is it also the ENORMOUS ATLANTIS ON THE BENT SHOULDERS OF THE PEASANTS?), Atlantis of Atlantis, a continent submerged under the weight of worlds, which words rich in sap will bring afloat again. LANGUAGE: American (wherever you got it — and I could spot Lear, at last, you may say, and I like to add, yes, *King Lear*, Melville's *King Lear*, the king whose bones and blood float and circulate in the wake of the Pequod): you are miles away from calculated effect, you must be relaxed then, or beginning to breathe rarified air, unpolluted discourse. LANGUAGE: a sermon of metaliterary order, language, quoted or unquoted, a puddingstone of exhilarating pathos = love = knowledge: your agglutinative style. Story: part two.

In this edifice I find three flaws: a) Certain chapters of a descriptive-naturalistic 'nature'; b) Haste; c) The fact that there is a conclusion. Towards the middle of the novel you go into a Nabokov County narrative. I know we spoke about this before, but I want to add something new; also I may have changed, slightly, if not opinion, at least intention. Benedetta finds herself caught between guyness and fertility. Also between New Jersey and the Bronx. That is Atlantis (tragedy by disappearance). Benedetta whose background, to continue the anthropological metaphor, is epitomized by Anabasis. You know my first reaction to this chapter. It still bugs me, but at the same time I do not (anymore) think that you have to eliminate, if not the chapter, the function that the chapter (or a series of chapters) might assume. Anabasis, in fact, is the place that you describe, but, that's exactly it; you want to do away with description, with sociology, and instead

237

consider it as meeting point of, again, fertility and sterility. This time, however, the two are not separated into two gangs of mafiosi, they rub each other within the desperation of one college. It is not a fact that many Anabasis girls go towards what they'd consider a genuine act of fertility (a fuck) as if their participation had been programed by a computer? They made even fucking a duty (Nabokov County, as you hint). But my point isn't made until I stretch what I just said into an invitation: this invitation: utilize Anabasis, because its heroine, Benedetta, is capable of finding in the Adonais myth (transfigured as it is, and nobody ever transfigured it so much as you have done) what her 'real' sister, you know the sister of flesh and bone as opposed to the fictional one (see good old Forster and all that jazz) what her 'real' sister might be looking for even at Anabasis. After all, do I understand correctly when I read that Crystal Baby, also from Anabasis, is rather well-adjusted with the guysters of New Jersey?

Do I talk structure? Do you mind? And if structure has any reason to exist in fluidity (Anaxagoras would say, yes, it does have a reason) then I would inject some new adrenaline into the withered limbs of sociological resentment. Literature can, must, do that. And I move on to the second flaw: Haste. This is of course a corollary. Its nature is psychological. Shall I call it my impression? Anyhow, some hortatory statements are all I can proffer, I guess. And what I mean is that you were right, when you said that the central chapters, again Anabasis and the Nabokov County biz, were to constitute a contrast, a musical sweetness, kind of Danube-like, to the jukebox (juke + Dylan + Marechiaro + scratch +

238

belch, even) quality of the first and third part, the latter being, of course a second coming, as you say, of Adonais, the Lord. Yes, you were G.D. right, only... Only, it seems to me, you were too hasty to strike, and you got your finger on the wrong key, that is to say you got mixed up in a kind of twilight which is not subversive enough. (Subversive twilight = you know, the good side of *gggozzano*, the best of Palazzeschi). I am sorry to insist. But the cookie in your hand is too appetizing for me to overlook the possibility of being honest. After all I'm talking about something which has not only filled me with pleasure, but also given me a totally different understanding of you, and the world you are investigating. Some more time, to conclude, will then help you find out the style you need to bring the contrast to full evidence and to obtain from such contrast not simply two parts at odds, but a third, self-logical, autonomous event. Time, I think, you also want to dedicate, to the third part: the return of J.A. Let me move on anyway. As regards the third indication: the problem of a conclusion (whether or not to point at one), I am not sure. It might be that I am too hung up on anthro, or too pessimistically juvenile to accept a pregnancy, but, for that matter, I would be bothered (and therefore optimistically juvenile) if there were no such thing. However as I said, I am not sure. This last remark may contain a great deal of bullshit: I'm just showing uneasiness, but would not want it to interfere with your story.

Third part of the story: recapitulation. I think you've got a jewel. I see what you mean when you refer to Joyce as your forefather. You're right. You both bring back mythopoiesis into language, the game of language, the only serious political game (commitment = imagination). *Benedetta* proves that first comes the VERBUM and then reality. As it normally happens in any miracle.

P.S. Giose, what follows must be added to my previous letter: I overlooked the fact of DISPLACE-MENT. That is *kiss* instead of *kill*, guyster instead of gangster, etc. It's excellent and, of course, more than a touch of cuteness. It has the quality (the taste) of Calvino's baron or better still of his Ursula X's, the girl who depilates while precipitating in vacuum before the world was made. I mean each writer is entitled to some displacement. One follows enlightenment and makes 'rationality' work on an absurd premise; others (you, Gadda, etc.) displace by semantic traps. Ultimately your game is more dangerous, less dainty, more spring-like, and above all perfectly functional, I believe, to the anthropological metaphor. It is thru displacement of semantic juice that I got juice (one type of juice) out of *Benedetta*.

16. A Novelist's Novel

The tenth, dated February, 1972, is by W.O. Perlmutter, a fascinating speaker, warm and friendly, the idealist with blue eyes. Wears wool suits.

Benedetta . . . is magnificent, a novelist's novel. Your use of language is superbly innovative and gracefully executed. The book also has much to say about life and literature in our time. You take the reader by the hand and with wit and satire lead him through mysterious places, purging hell with laughter. The book deserves close reading, just as *Ulysses* did.

17. Poetry

The eleventh, dated 1 febbraio, is by Silvana Coen, mother of two, tense and intense at times, suave most of the time, collects precious old objects, often leaves the City for nostalgia of her house in the Country, after which she leaves the Country for nostalgia of her house in the City. Her letter is in Italian.

. . . Questa mattina ho cercato di telefonarti in ufficio ma mi hanno trasferita dal 4573300 al 4578400 senza fortuna. Il tuo numero di casa non è elencato per cui eccomi qua a dirti che sto leggendo *Benedetta in Guysterland* con ammirazione, invidia.

Tu parli di questa tua opera come di un romanzo sperimentale, di una satira del sesso e del costume. E questa c'è ed è efficacissima. Hai, per esempio, satireggiando, distrutto la mafia come 'le forze dell'ordine'. Ma quello che mi affascina nel tuo libro è la poesia, liquida questa si, che penetra, entra, esce, rientra nei tuoi concetti espressi con tanta ricchezza di linguaggio e di immagini. Io, che sono in un periodo di 'secca', ti invidio (cum amore) la carica di vitalità che traduci in parole, frasi, poesia quasi rabbiosamente, come un fiume in piena. Riandando attraverso le tue lettere traggo, però, un incoraggiamento che, forse, mi aiuterà a superare questa crisi di coscienza che mi paralizza.

Incontrerai amiche più inconsistenti e turbate di me, ma certo non più ammirate dal tuo talento.

18. The Rage of the Age

The twelfth, dated March 5, is by John di Palma, a man who sold me a house while I was swimming in a motel swimming pool, for the sake of having me as a neighbor of his, I guess. A huge man who received a master's degree from Columbia, reads dirty books, buys and sells properties endlessly, and after dinner sleeps soundly.

Giose Rimanelli has taken his licence and zoomed through all of the red lights and broken all of the codes and modes. His book is a Totem Pole among a sea of limp pricks.

His simulation of the Guyster Lichen has made him a master of lichenology in a literary sense. The reader has a definite feeling of potent pubic problems; parasitic, paranoiac, paramagnetic, partially parasynthetic but definitely a paratactic journey through a liquid abstract locality where only a creative geni can pull out the stops, mold the flow and bring the fungi back to life.

Fee-Fie-Fo-Fumm — I smell the cud of an Italian. Not Joe Adonis, but Zip Rimanelli who will go down in history as the one who DID IT. He did it with his head, balls and fingers. It will be the rage of the age, the thrill of the shill, the prize of the wise, but riches he won't gain because the Rot of a plot the people dot.

19. A Peculiar Kind of Insight

The thirteenth, dated March 6, 1972, is by Leslie A. Fiedler, author of the controversial and famed Love and Death in the American Novel, a kind, smiling man with a rough whitish beard, and the heart of an adolescent.

I'm sending back your manuscript with this. It gave me much pleasure, and I think it would be a great loss to all of us if you did not become an American novelist at this point.

I think there is always a peculiar kind of insight into the nature of a language which one acquires later in life. Besides that, the series of puns on which your book depends for its effect have a special sharpness because of your closeness to and distance from the American language. I am grateful that you gave me a chance to see your manuscript, and I am looking forward to talking with you further in Italy as well as here.

I had a chance to go through the poems too — which I somehow think moved me more than the prose (seem closer to where your wit and passion are in equal balance). I like especially those poems which move towards reminiscence and narrative — especially the Bella Carnap one.

20. Feelings and Sensations

The last one, dated March 20, 1972, is by the perfect typist of Benedetta, Laraine Rowe, a blond young woman who sits at the typewriter with a firmly arched back as the courtly lady of old presiding over the dinner table.

Few things can be as difficult as the attempt to give a 'solid' reaction to the essentially fluid experience of a 'liquid' novel. As I've already mentioned to you, the first few chapters disoriented me.

Yet, I was drawn into the novel by its alternating current, of feelings and sensations, that add patchwork insight into the word-world which is Benedetta's perception of reality.

Dominating the unreal fantasy world of guy Mafiosi who utter words out of the mouths of Shakespeare and others, in their TV plots to 'kiss' the enemy, is the reality of Benedetta herself, a girl who, in trying to escape from her Puritan Nabokov County background, finds that it is a part of everything she touches. Her eventual insanity, though not easy to accept, may be one of the few choices for someone unable to cope with the 'way of the word-world'.

21. From the Chequer'd Shade Garden

Following the readers' indications, I made slight revisions in the manuscript, chopping down here and there (yes, the Nabokov County scenes, and episodes about Benedetta's father), and adding, here and there, sentences. I penned out most four letter words, and the obscene.

Basically, the manuscript remains the same. It could be read by a child.

A few answers were written almost as reviews of the book, and rather than to me, they were addressed, it seems, to a prospective editor. They sponsor the book, and want it to be in print. Alas, stillness becoming alive, yet still? Yes, be still. Wait. On the shelves of the bathroom; where I see words as figures walking in a chequer'd shade.

Yet the problem of words walking is nothing else than the eternal problem of confrontation, of conflict, between man and destiny. There is a difference between the material world and that which we experience, since the material world must be filtered through our minds before we become conscious of it. Therefore, we know nothing but our individual selves. Our own consciousness interprets itself in terms of what we have bestowed on the material or on a particular event. We try to find an identity only by means of this projection, that is in relation to something: rhythm, pure order, primitive ritual. A predominant factor in Greek tragedy is its use of the chorus and of the rhythmic exchange between the players. I'm talking about the abstract, and about that Art that is not experience but an order that is created out of the imagination, and not dependent on experience. The words, therefore, rhythm, is a search to be, and to break out of one's temporal prison.

What I didn't say to my readers is how I went on fishing this way. It started some time ago, with Anthony Burgess. He wrote a nice introduction to my first book of English poems, titled *Alien*, which I forgot to take down from the shelves of my bathroom to show to a publisher, also because immediately after that I nearly smashed my brain in a car accident. Just before the accident, however, I had time to answer Anthony Burgess in a letter . . . which I never sent. And after the accident I started with *Benedetta*. That letter thus, being a fishing prelude, I now dedicate to all *Benedetta* readers.

22. The Letter

Thank you, my friends. For you did share. And I did dare to share. Now, now. Do we deserve this state? Nor would we love at lower rate. Thus, though we cannot make the sun stand still we are able to make him run. And a little child shall lead them. But, of course, you can knock forever on a deaf man's door. Always it brings everything back, for that is where the battle must be fought.

The WORD, after all, is not the prerequisite of scholars and critics and historians. It is yours and mine — our freehold and our possession. What does it matter? One way or another, in pretense or in sincerity. Little girls are made of sugar and spice and everything nice. Truly, truly. Unless a grain of wheat falls into the earth and dies, it remains alone. But if it dies, it bears much fruit.

Plink, plink, plink. Nickels! What do you call them, WORDS? What's a word? An apple. And an apple? A thirst to bite. And a bite? A kite. We lost many kites, this year. And what remains is how to regulate genetic projects. The time when you can buy babies frozen in the supermarket. Embryo infants. Infinitely worse than a cartilage sitting by a tree stump long after dark. Should we eat only for nourishment but for pleasure too? All written warranties or guarantees would have to be expressed in simple and readily understood language. Though he invented electrical appliances, and the heavy rain also who goes with me, climbing the buildings, kicking the football.

But you know. They only lead into a world where all things are possible and nothing sure. Or the Holy Grail. A question which postulates that there is no answer. An answer for which there was no question. Neither the Fisher-King. The syntagmatic chain. The recognition of metonymy on the recognition of contiguity. *Perchè chi arriva non conta affatto. I primi sono sempre ammazzati. Io.*

Povera vacca. In fact, we walk. Or rest. A dream has power, anyway. To poison the sleep. Or we rise. One wandering thought that pollutes the day. A kind of careless, shoestring in whose tie I see a wild civility. Imprisoned behind the icy glass windows of your eyes.

Moodslength? I don't understand. This bird-house is going to be for sparrows only. Because evil becomes a spent force when we put up no re-sistance. You stupid darkness!

Then, well. What's a WORD? An apple. And an apple? A thirst to bite. And a bite? A kite. We didn't lose any kites this year, after all. Even if what re-mains is how to get the most out of your water bed. Alien to my senses. Because I know only that I'm looking for pebbles. Though soon it was winter then spring then summer.

About the Author

Giose Rimanelli was born on November 28, 1926, in Casacalenda, Italy, of an Italian father and a Canadian mother. He gained international repute with some of his novels during the fifties, some of which are *The Day of the Lion* (1954), *Original Sin* (1957), *Third Class Ticket* (1958), *A Social Position* (1959).

To his narrative activity he has added poetry, professional journalism, theater and literary criticism both in Italian and in English. As for poetry, Giose Rimanelli has primarily engaged himself with Latin and Provençal poets whom he has translated, acquiring a style of his own.

One of his Italian-language novels, *Tiro al piccione* (1953, 1991), was made into a film by director Giuliano Montaldo in 1961.

He has lived in the United States since 1960, and has taught Italian and Comparative Literature at New York University, Yale University, the University of British Columbia, the University of California at Los Angeles, and the State University of New York at Albany. He is SUNY-Albany Professor Emeritus.

By the Same Author

Tiro al piccione (1953, 1991)
The Day of the Lion (1954)
Original Sin (1957)
Third Class Ticket (1958)
A Social Position (1959)
The Sneak Craft (1959)
Tea at Picasso's (1961)
Lares (1962)
The French Horn (1962)
Modern Canadian Stories (1966)
Carmina blabla (1967)
Love Monks of the Middle Ages (1967)
Tragic America (1968)
Poems Make Pictures, Pictures Make Poems (1971)
Graffiti (1977)
Italian Literature: Roots and Branches (1978)
Molise Molise (1979)
Time Hidden Between Lines (1986)
Arcano (1990)
Moliseide (1990, 1992)